Jack Winters' Baseball Team; or, The Rivals of the Diamond

Mark Overton

Jack tried to keep the boy's head above water

JACK WINTERS'
BASEBALL TEAM

OR,

The Rivals of the Diamond

BY

MARK OVERTON

1919

CONTENTS

CHAPTER I
THREE BOYS OF CHESTER

"No use talking, Toby, there's something on Jack's mind of late, and it's beginning to bother him a lot, I think!"

"Well, Steve, you certainly give me the creeps, that's what you do, with your mysterious hints of all sorts of trouble hanging over our heads, just as they say the famous sword of that old worthy, Damocles, used to hang by a single hair, ready to fall. Look here, do you realize, Steve, what it would mean if Jack went and got himself rattled *just now*?"

"Huh! guess I do that, Toby, when, for one thing, we're scheduled to go up against that terrible Harmony nine day after tomorrow."

"And if Jack is getting cold feet already, on account of something or other, I can see our finish now, Steve."

"Still, we beat them in that first great game, don't let's forget that, Toby, and take what consolation we can from the fact."

"Oh! rats! we know how that came about. They'd never been beaten the entire season by any team in the county, and had grown a bit careless. Because they had a clean record they believed they could just about wipe up the ground with poor old Chester, a slow town that up to this year had never done anything worth while in connection with boys' outdoor sports."

"That's right, Toby. Never will I forget how humiliated I felt when they struck town on that glorious day. They came in a lot of cars and motor-trucks, with the Harmony Band playing, 'Lo, the Conquering Hero Comes,' and with whoops and toots galore from the crowds of faithful rooters. Why, bless you, they felt so confident of winning that they even left their star battery at home to rest up, and used the second string slab-team. But, oh! my eye! it was a saddened lot of Harmony fellows that wended their way back home, everybody trying to explain what had struck them to the tune of eleven to five. Wow!"

"Great Cæsar! Steve, but didn't old Chester go crazy that same night, though, with the bonfires making the sky look red, and the boys yelling through the main streets in a serpentine procession, carrying Jack on their shoulders? The campus in front of the high school was packed solid when Professor Yardley made a speech, and

1

congratulated our gallant team because we had that same day put Chester once for all on the map!"

"But, shucks! Toby, the tables were sure turned on us when we went over to play that second game. Those chaps were on their toes that day, and it was Hendrix and Chase, their star battery, that fed us of their best."

"Yes, we did lose, all right, but don't forget that we fought tooth and nail to the very last."

"Say, that rally in the ninth was a thrilling piece of business, wasn't it, Toby? Why, only for our right fielder, Big Bob Jeffries, hitting that screamer straight into the hands of the man playing deep centre instead of lifting it over his head for a homer, we'd have won out. There were two on bases, you remember, with the score three to four."

"Now we're tied, with one game each to our credit, and Harmony coming over the day after tomorrow to take our measure, they boast. Jack has been so confident ever since he picked up that new pitcher, Donohue, on the sand lots in town, that I'm puzzled a heap to know what ails him latterly."

"One thing sure, Toby, Jack is bound to speak up sooner or later, and let his two chums know what's in the wind. I rather expect he agreed to meet us here today so as to have a heart-to-heart talk; and if so, it's bound to be about the matter that's troubling him."

"I certainly hope so, because when you know the worst you can plan to meet the difficulty. And if only we could win the rubber in this series with Harmony, it'd make little old Chester famous."

The two boys who were holding this animating and interesting conversation stood kicking their heels on a corner where the main street in the town was crossed by another. It was about ten o'clock on a morning in early summer. Chester seemed to be quite a bustling sort of town, located in the East. Considerable business was carried on in the place, for there were several factories running, employing hundreds of workers at good wages.

Certainly no town in the broad land could be more advantageously located than the borough in which Toby Hopkins and Steve Mullane lived. It lay close to the shore of Lake Constance, a beautiful sheet of clear water three miles across at its broadest point, and at least twelve long, with many deep and really mysterious coves, and also bordered by quite a stretch of swampy land toward the south. Far up toward its northern extremity lay the Big Woods, where during winters considerable lumbering was done by a concern that had a camp there.

As if that wonderful sheet of water were not enough to gratify the tastes of all boys who loved to skate and swim and fish and go boating, there was Paradise River emptying into the lake close by, a really picturesque stream with its puzzling bends and constantly novel views that burst upon the sight as one drove a canoe up its lazy current of a sunny summer afternoon.

Toby was a character. He had an enviable disposition in that he seldom if ever showed a temper. His many peculiarities really endeared him to his boy friends. As he was apt to say when introducing himself to some newcomer in town, "My name is Hopkins, 'Hop' for short; and that's why they put me at short on the diamond; because I rather guess I can *hop* to beat the band, if I can't do much else."

But in Chester, it was well known among the admirers of the new baseball team, that by his "hopping" Toby managed to cover short as few fellows could. Seldom did the most erratic hit get past those nimble hands of his, that could stab a vicious stinging ball coming straight from the bat of a slugger, and apparently tagged for a two-bagger at least.

Steve Mullane was of heavier build, and admirably suited for his position of catcher. He usually proved himself well worthy of the warm regard of Chester's rooting fans, who flocked to the games these days.

And yet, Chester, now baseball mad apparently, had, until this season, seemed to be wrapped in a regular Rip Van Winkle sleep of twenty years, in so far as outdoor sports for boys went. Time and again there had been a sporadic effort made to enthuse the school lads in baseball, football, hockey, and such things, but something seemed lacking in the leadership, and all the new schemes died soon after they came on the carpet.

Then a little event happened that put new life and "ginger" into the whole town, so far as the boys were concerned. A new boy arrived in Chester, and his name it happened was Jack Winters. From the very start it seemed as though Jack must have been meant for a natural-born leader among his fellows. They liked him for his genial ways, and soon began to ask his opinion with regard to almost everything that came along. During the preceding winter, Jack had started

3

several things that turned out to be extremely successful. Rival hockey teams once more contested on the smooth ice of the frozen lake; also one or two iceboats were seen skimming over the great expanse of Constance, something that had not been known in half a generation.

The backward boys of Chester began to talk as though big notions might be gripping them. If other towns no larger than the one in which they lived had gymnasiums, and regularly organized field clubs, with splendid grounds for athletic meets, what was to hinder them from doing the same?

So in due time a new baseball team was organized, consisting not only of those who attended Chester High, but several fellows who worked in the factories, but had Saturday afternoons off. They had practiced strenuously, and under a coach who had been quite a famous player in one of the big leagues, until a broken leg put him out of business; Joe Hooker was now working in one of the factories, though just as keen at sports as ever.

When, earlier in the season, Chester actually walked away with two games in succession from the pretty strong team at Marshall, the good people awakened to the fact that a revolution had indeed taken place in the boys of the town. A new spirit and ambition pervaded every heart. Doing things worth while is the best way to arouse a boy to a consciousness that he has a fighting chance.

From what passed between Toby and Steve as they waited for their chum to join them, it can be seen that great things were hanging in the balance those days. In about forty-eight hours Harmony would be swarming into the town riding in all manner of conveyances, shouting and showing every confidence in the ability of their great team to take that deciding game.

There was good need of anxiety in the Chester camp. Not once had Harmony gone down to defeat all season until that unlucky day when, scorning the humble newly organized Chester nine, they had come over with a patched-up team to "go through the motions," as one of them had sadly confessed while on the way home after losing.

Ten minutes later and Toby gave an exclamation of satisfaction.

"Here comes Jack!" he told his companion, and immediately both glued their eyes on the clean-limbed and bright-faced young fellow who was swinging toward them, waving a hand as he caught their signals.

There was nothing remarkable about Jack Winters, save that he seemed a born athlete, had a cheery, winning way about him, and seemed to have a magnetism such as all born leaders, from Napoleon down, possess, that drew others to him, and made them believe in his power for extracting victory from seeming defeat.

"Sorry to have kept you waiting so long, fellows," Jack remarked, as he joined them, "but a man stopped me on the street, and his business was of such importance that I couldn't break away in a hurry. But let's adjourn to a quieter place; over there in the little park under the trees I can see a bench that's empty. I've got something to tell you that nobody must hear except you two."

"Does it have a bearing on the great game with Harmony, Jack?" begged Toby, who was a bit impatient after his way.

"It may mean everything to us in that battle!" Jack admitted, as he headed for the bench in the small park.

CHAPTER II
A WEAK LINK IN THE CHAIN

When Jack dropped down on the bench, the others crowded as close up on either side as they could possibly get. No one was near by, save a couple of nursemaids chatting and gossiping while they trundled their baby carriages back and forth; and they were too much engrossed in exchanging views of the gallant policeman on the block to notice three boys with their heads close together, "plotting mischief," as they would doubtless believe.

"Now break loose and give us a hint what it's all about, please, Jack!" urged Toby.

"Because both of us have noticed that something's been bothering you latterly," added Steve; "and as you're not the fellow to borrow trouble it's got us guessing, I tell you. Who's the weak brother on the team you're afraid of, Jack?"

"I see your guessing has been in the right direction, Steve," the other went on to remark, with an affectionate nod; for in the few months he had known them, these new chums had won a warm place in Jack Winters' heart. "Don't be startled now when I tell you it's Fred who's keeping me awake nights."

Both the others uttered low exclamations of surprise.

"What! Fred Badger, our bully reliable third baseman, equal to that crackerjack Harmony boasts about as the best in the State!" gasped Toby. "Why, only yesterday I heard you say our Fred was getting better right along, and that his equal couldn't be easily found. We don't even need to keep a substitute back of Fred, his work is that gilt-edged."

"That's just what's troubling me," admitted Jack, quietly. "If I was able to lay my hand on some one right now who could fill Fred's shoes even fairly well, I wouldn't be so bothered; but there isn't a boy in Chester who can play that difficult position so as not to leave a terrible gap in our stone-wall infield, no one but Fred."

"But what's the matter with Fred?" demanded Steve.

"I saw him not an hour ago," spoke up Toby, "and say, he didn't look so *very* sick then, let me tell you, Jack. He was swallowing an ice-cream soda in the drug-store, and seemed to be enjoying it immensely, too."

"And yet," added Steve, thoughtfully, "now that you mention it, Jack, seems to me Fred *has* been acting a little queer lately. There's been a sort of shifting way he avoids looking straight into your eyes when you're talking with him. Why, when I got speaking about our next big game, and hoped he'd play like a regular demon at third sack he grinned sheepishly, and simply said he meant to try and do himself credit, but nobody could ever tell how luck was going to pan out."

Jack shook his head.

"That's just it, fellows," he went on to say, gloomily. "I've heard the same thing from others. In fact, Phil Parker even went on to say it looked like Fred was getting ready to excuse himself in case he did commit some terrible crime in juggling a ball when a vital time in the game came, and a clean throw meant win or lose."

"I'd hate to see that spirit shown under any conditions," said Jack, "because it means lack of confidence, and such a thing has lost no end of games. It's the fellow who says he can and will do things that comes in ahead nearly every time. But listen, boys, that isn't the worst of this thing."

"Gee whiz! what's coming now, Jack?" asked Toby, wriggling uneasily on the bench.

"Of course you know that over in Harmony, which is a larger place than Chester, there is quite a sporting element," Jack continued. "Latterly, we've been told quite an interest has been aroused in the outcome of this deciding game between the two rival clubs; and that some rich sports from the city have even come up to make wagers on the result. I've heard gentlemen here tell this, and deplore the fact that such a thing could invade an innocent sport like baseball. You both know this, don't you, fellows?"

"Yes," said Steve, quickly, "I've heard a lot of talk about it, and how they are determined to arrest anybody making an open bet on the game at the grounds when the crowd is there; but even that isn't going to prevent the laying of wagers in secret."

"I ran across a Harmony fellow yesterday," Toby now remarked, eagerly, "and he said there was a terrible lot of excitement over there about this game. You see, the news about our new pitcher has leaked out, from the Chester boys doing considerable bragging; and they're going to play their very best to win against us. He also admitted that there was open betting going on, with heavy odds on Harmony."

7

Jack sighed.

"That all agrees with what came to me in a side way," he explained. "In other words, the way things stand, there will be a big lot of money change hands in case Harmony does win. And those sporting men who came up from the city wouldn't think it out of the way to pay a good fat *bribe* if they could make sure that some player on the Chester team would throw the game, in case it began to look bad for Harmony!"

Toby almost fell off his seat on hearing Jack say that.

"My stars! and do you suspect Fred of entering into such a base conspiracy as that would be, Jack?" he demanded, hoarsely; while Steve held his very breath as he waited for the other to reply.

"Remember, not one word of this to a living soul," cautioned Jack; "give me your solemn promise, both of you, before I say anything more."

Both boys held up a right hand promptly.

"I never blab anything, even in my sleep, Jack," said Steve; "and until you give permission never a single word will I pass along."

"Same here," chirped Toby; "I'll put a padlock on my lips right away, and wild horses couldn't force me to leak. Now tell us what makes you suspect poor old Fred of such a horrible crime?"

"I've tried to make myself believe it impossible," Jack commenced; "and yet all the while I could see that Fred has changed in the last ten days, changed in lots of ways. There's something been bothering him, that's plain."

"Stop a minute, will you, Jack, and let me say something," interrupted Toby. "I wouldn't mention it even to you fellows only for this thing coming up. I chance to know why Fred has been looking worried of late. Shall I tell you, in hopes that it might ease your mind, Jack?"

"Go on, Toby," urged Steve. "We ought to get at the bottom of this thing before it's too late, and the mischief done. Any player can throw a game, if he's so minded, and the opportunity comes to him, and mebbe not even be suspected; but as a rule, baseball players are far too honorable to attempt such tricks."

"It's a secret over at our house," Toby went on to say. "My mother happens to know that Doctor Cooper told Mrs. Badger she could be a well woman again if only she went to a hospital in the city, and submitted to an operation at the hands of a noted surgeon he recommended. But they are poor, you know, boys, and it's next to impossible for them to ever think of raising the three hundred dollars the operation would cost. She told my mother Fred was making himself fairly sick over his inability to do something to earn that big sum. So you see the poor chap has had plenty of reason for looking glum lately."

"I knew nothing about Fred's mother being sick," Jack admitted; "and I'm sorry to learn it now; but don't you see, your explanation only seems to make matters all the blacker for him, Toby?"

"Why, how can that be, Jack?"

"Only this, that while Fred might never be bribed to listen to any scheme to throw the game in favor of Harmony, on his own account, the tempting bait of three hundred dollars might win him over now, because of his love for his mother."

"But, Jack, however could he explain where he got so much money?" cried Steve. "It would come out, and he'd be called on for an explanation. Even his mother would refuse to touch a cent dishonestly gained, though she died for it. Why, Fred would be crazy to think he could get away with such a game."

"Still, he might be blind to that fact," Jack explained. "The one thing before his eyes would be that he could pick up the money so sorely needed, and for which he might even be tempted to barter his honor. All sorts of explanations could be made up to tell where he got the cash. But there's even something more than that to make matters look bad for Fred."

"As what, Jack?" begged Toby, breathlessly.

"Just day before yesterday," the other continued, "I chanced to pass along over yonder, and glancing across saw Fred sitting on this very bench. He was so busy talking with a man that he never noticed me. That man was a stranger in Chester, at least I had never seen him before. Yes, and somehow it struck me there was a bit of a sporty look about his appearance!"

"Gee whiz! the plot thickens, and that does look black for Fred, I must say," grunted Toby, aghast.

"I was interested to the extent of hanging around to watch them further," Jack went on to say, "and for half an hour they continued to sit here, all the while talking. I thought the sporty stranger glanced around a number of times, as though he didn't want any one to overhear a word of what he was saying. He seemed to have a paper of some sort, too, which I saw Fred signing. I wondered then if he could be such a simpleton as to attach his name to any dishonorable deal; but sometimes even the sharpest fellow shows a weak point. Now I know that Fred must be fairly wild to get hold of a certain sum of money, it makes me more afraid than ever he is pledged to toss away the game, if it looks as though Chester is going to win out on a close margin."

"Then we ought to drop Fred out, and take our medicine with another man on third," proposed Steve, hotly.

"I'd do that in a minute, and take no chances of foul play," said Jack, "if only we knew of anybody capable of filling his shoes. If Harmony knows a weak player covers third bag, they'll make all their plays revolve around him, that's sure. The only thing I can see is to let Fred keep on, and hope the game will not be so close that he could lose it for Chester by a bad break. Besides that I could have a heart-to-heart talk with him, not letting him see that we suspected his loyalty, but impressing it on his mind that every fellow in the team believed in him to the utmost, and that we'd be broken-hearted if anything happened to lose us this game on which the whole future of clean sport in Chester hangs."

"That might do it, Jack!" snapped Toby, eagerly. "You've got a way about you that few fellows can resist. Yes, that's our only plan, it seems; Fred is indispensable on the team at this late stage, when a sub couldn't be broken in, even if we had one handy, which we haven't. Play him at his regular position, and let's hope there'll be no chance for double-dealing on his part."

"But we'll all be mighty anxious as the game goes along, believe me," asserted Steve, as they arose to leave the vicinity of the bench. "I'll be skimpy with my throws to third to catch a runner napping, for fear Fred might make out to fumble and get the ball home just too late to nab the runner. And, Jack, try your level best to convince Fred that the eyes of all Chester will be on him during that game, with his best girl, pretty Molly Skinner, occupying a front seat in the grand stand!"

CHAPTER III
THE LAST PRACTICE GAME

On the following morning, twice Jack walked around to where the humble cottage of the Badger family stood, on purpose to call on Fred, and have a chat with him; but on each occasion missed seeing the third baseman. His mother Jack had never met before, and he was quite interested in talking with her. Purposely Jack influenced her to speak of Fred, and his ambitions in the world. He could see that, like most mothers, she was very proud of her eldest son, and had an abiding faith in his ability to accomplish great things when later on he took his place in business circles.

She had been a widow for some years. The house was very tidy, and a pretty flower and vegetable garden spoke well for Fred's early rising and assiduous labors as a young provider. When Jack purposely mentioned that he had heard something about her anticipating a visit to the city to spend a little while at a hospital, she shook her head sadly, and a look of pain crossed her careworn face as she said:

"Dr. Cooper wants me to go and see his friend, who is a famous surgeon, but I'm afraid the cost is much more than I can afford at present, unless some miracle comes up before long. But I try to forget my troubles, and feel that I have much to be thankful for in my three children, all so healthy and so clever. Why, there's hardly a thing Fred wouldn't do for me. Ah! if only his father could have lived to see him now, how proud he would be of such a boy!"

When Jack came away after that little interesting talk, he felt very down-hearted. What a shock it would be to his fond mother should she ever be forced to learn that her boy had taken money from those who were betting on the outcome of the great game, in order to betray his comrades who placed the most implicit confidence in his loyalty.

Even though it were done with the best motive in the world, that of trying to make his mother a well woman again, she would bitterly regret his having yielded to such an ignoble temptation and fallen so low as to sell a game.

Then came the last practice that afternoon, to prepare for the morrow, when Harmony's confident hosts would come with brooms waving, to indicate how they meant to sweep up the ground with poor Chester's best offering.

Coach Hooker was on deck, for already the spirit of newly awakened sport had permeated the whole place, so that the boss at his factory gladly released him from duty for that special afternoon, in order that the Chester boys might profit from his sage advice.

Fred did not show up until just before the game with the scrub team was being called, so that of course Jack could not find an opportunity just then to indulge in any side talk with the keeper of the third sack. He determined not to let anything prevent his walking home in company with Fred, however, and trying to see behind the mask which he believed the other was wearing to conceal the real cause of his uneasiness.

The game started and progressed, with every fellow filled with vim and vigor. To those who had come to size up the team before the great battle, it seemed as if every member had made strides forward since the last match, when Harmony won out in that last fierce inning after the rally that almost put Chester on top.

From time to time, each, individual player would seem to rise up and perform the most remarkable stunts. Now it was Joel Jackman, out in center, who made a marvelous running catch, jumping in the air, and pulling down a ball that seemed good for at least a three-bagger, also holding the horse-hide sphere even while he rolled over twice on the ground.

Later on, a great triple play was pulled off, Winters at first to Jones on second, and home to Mullane in time to catch a runner attempting to profit by all this excitement. Such a wonderful handling of the ball in a match game would give the crowd a chance to break loose with mighty cheers, friends and foes joining in to do the clever athletes honor.

Then there was Big Bob Jeffries, a terror at the bat; three times up, and each occasion saw him almost knock the cover off the ball, making two home runs, and a three-bagger in the bargain. Why, if only Big Bob could duplicate that performance on the following day, it was "good-night to Harmony." But then there was a slight difference between the pitcher of the scrub team and the mighty slab artist who officiated for Harmony; and possibly, Bob might only find thin air when he struck savagely at the oncoming ball, dexterously tagged for a drop, or a sweeping curve.

Nevertheless, everybody seemed satisfied that the entire team was "on edge," and in the "pink of condition." If they failed to carry off the honors in that deciding game, there would be no valid excuse to offer, save that Harmony was a shade too much for them. Even though they might be defeated, they meant to fight doggedly to the end of the ninth inning, and feel that they had given the champions of the county a "run for their money."

Win or lose, Chester had awakened to the fact that the local team was well worth patronizing. Another season would see vast improvements, and the time might yet come when Chester would write her name at the top of the county teams. All sorts of other open-air sports were being talked of, and there was a host of eager candidates ready to apply for every sort of position. Jack Winters had managed to awaken the sleepy town, and "start things humming," most fellows admitted, being willing to give him the greater part of the credit.

So when the game was ended, the players gathered around Joe Hooker to listen to his frank criticisms, and pledge themselves anew to do their level best to "take Harmony's scalp" on the morrow.

Jack kept on the watch, and both Toby and Steve saw what he was aiming at when he hurriedly left the group and walked quickly after Fred, who had started toward home.

"Only hope he makes his point," muttered Toby to the other. "Fred certainly played like a fiend today. Nothing got by him, you noticed. He scooped that hummer from Bentley's bat off the ground as neat as wax. No professional could have done better, I heard Joe Hooker say. He thinks Fred is a jim-dandy at third, and that he's a natural ball player, strong at the bat, as well as in the field."

Meanwhile, Jack had overtaken Fred, who, hearing his footsteps, turned his head to see who might be hurrying after him. Jack fancied he looked a trifle confused at seeing the captain of the team trying to come up with him, though that might only be imagination, after all. Still, doubtless Fred's mother must have mentioned the fact that Jack had been at the house twice that morning, as though he had something of importance to communicate.

"I'm going your way, it happens, this afternoon, Fred," Jack remarked as he came up, "as I have an errand over at your neighbor, Mrs. Jennings, a commission for my mother; so I'll step alongside, and we can chat a bit as we walk along."

"Glad to have your company, Jack," said Fred; but all the same he did not seem so *very* enthusiastic over it. "The boys all worked like a well-oiled machine today, I noticed, and if only we can do as well in the big game, we ought to have a look in, I should think."

13

"We've just *got* to make up our minds we mean to win that game tomorrow, no matter how Hendrix pitches gilt-edged ball," Jack told him. "Every fellow must tell himself in the start that he will let nothing whatever interfere with his giving Chester of his very best. I don't care what it may be that stands in the way, we must brush it aside, and fight together to carry the day. Why, Chester will just go crazy if only we can down the boasting team that has never tasted defeat this season up to that fluke game, when they underestimated the fighting qualities of the rejuvenated Chester nine. And we can do it, Fred, we surely can, if only we pull together in team work, and every fellow stands on his honor to do his level best. You believe that, don't you, Fred?"

The other looked at Jack, and a slight gleam, as of uncertainty, began to show itself in his eyes. Then he shut his jaws together, and hurriedly replied:

"Of course I do, Jack. I'm not the one to show the white feather at such an early stage of the game. They've never accused *me* of having cold feet, no matter how bad things seemed to be breaking for my side. In fact, I've been a little proud of the reputation I have of being able to keep everlastingly at it. Stubbornness is my best hold, I've sometimes thought."

"Glad to know it, Fred, because that's a quality badly needed in baseball players. There's always hope up to the time the last man is down. Joe Hooker tells lots of wonderful stories of games he's seen won with two out in the ninth frame, and the other side half a dozen runs to the good. You are never beaten until the third man is out in the last inning. I'm glad to hear you say you mean to fight as never before in your life to get that game for the home club. Fact is, Fred, old fellow, I've been a little anxious about you latterly, because I thought you seemed upset over something or other, and I was afraid it might interfere with your play."

Fred started plainly, and shot Jack a quick look out of the corner of his eye, just as though he might be asking himself how much the other knew, or suspected.

"Well, the fact of the matter is, Jack, I have been feeling down-spirited over something. It's a family matter, and I hope you'll excuse me for not going into particulars just now. Day and night I seem to be wrestling with a problem that's mighty hard to solve; but there's a little ray of sunlight beginning to crop up, I don't mind telling you, and perhaps I'll find a way yet to weather the storm. I'm trying to feel cheerful about it; and you can depend on me taking care of third sack tomorrow the best I know how."

"That's all I can ask of any man, Fred; do yourself credit. Thousands of eyes will watch every move that is made, and among them those we care for most of every one in the whole world. I heard Molly Skinner saying this afternoon that she wouldn't miss that game for all the candy in the world. She also said she had a favorite seat over near third, and would go early so as to secure it. A brilliant play over *your* way would please Molly a heap, I reckon, Fred."

The other turned very red in the face, and then, tried to laugh it off as he hastened to say in a voice that trembled a little, despite his effort to control it:

"Yes, she told me the same thing, Jack, and it was nice of Molly to say it, for you know she's the prettiest girl in Chester, and a dozen boys are always hanging around her. Yes, I'd be a fool not to do myself proud tomorrow, with so many of my friends looking on; though of course any fellow might run into a bit of bad judgment and make a foozle, when he'd give five years of his life to work like a machine. I'm hoping, and praying, too, Jack, that such a streak of bad luck won't come my way, that's all I can say. Here's where I leave you, if you're bound for Jennings' place. If it's my promise to do my level best tomorrow you want, Jack, you've got it!"

So they parted. Still, Jack was not altogether easy in his mind. He went over every little incident of their recent intercourse as they trudged along side by side; and wondered whether Fred, who was not very well known to him, could be deceiving him. He cudgeled his brain to understand what those strange actions of the third baseman could mean, and who that sporty looking individual, whom he had with his own eyes seen talking so mysteriously to Fred might be.

CHAPTER IV
WHEN CHESTER AWAKENED

"Did you ever see such an enormous crowd?"

"Beats everything that ever happened around Chester all hollow!"

"Talk to me about excitement, the old town has gone stark, staring crazy over baseball; and it's all owing to Jack Winters coming to Chester, and shaking the dry bones of what used to be a Sleepy Hollow place."

"Right you are, Pete, and this is only a beginning of the glorious things scheduled to happen within the next six months or so. Already there's great talk about a football eleven that will clean up things in this neighborhood. We've got the right sort of stuff to make up a strong team, too, remember."

"And, Oliver, when I hear them speak of ice hockey, and skating for prizes, it gives me a heap of satisfaction, for you know I'm a crank on winter sports. Because the boys of Chester didn't seem to enthuse over such things has been the grief of my heart. But this day was certainly made for a thrilling baseball game."

"Oh! the sky looks blue enough, and that sun is some hot, I admit, but somehow I don't exactly like the looks of yonder bank of clouds that keeps hanging low-down close to the horizon in the southwest. We get most of our big storms from that quarter, don't forget."

A burst of derisive boyish laughter greeted this remark from the fellow named Oliver, who apparently was a bit of a pessimist, one of those who, while admitting that a day might be nearly perfect, chose to remember it was apt to be a weather-breeder, and bound to be followed by stormy times.

"Listen to the old croaker, will you?" one Chester rooter called out. "How anybody could pick a flaw with this splendid day beats me all hollow. Why, it was made on purpose for Chester to lick that boasting Harmony team, and send them back home like dogs, with their tails between their legs. Hurrah for Chester! Give the boys a cheer, fellows, because there they come on the field."

There was a wild burst of shouts from a myriad of boyish throats, and school flags, as well as other kinds, were waved from the grandstand where most of the town girls sat, until the whole wooden affair seemed a riot of color in motion.

The boys set to work passing the ball, and calling to one another as though they were full of business and confidence. Those in the audience who knew considerable about games felt that at least none of the home team suffered from stage fright. It looked promising. Evidently Jack Winters had managed to instill his nine with a fair degree of his own bubbling animation. They certainly looked fit to do their best in honor of their native town.

There were hosts of the Harmony folks over. They had come, and still arrived, in all sorts of conveyances, from private cars to stages and carryalls; and from the great row they kicked up with their calls and school cries, one might think it was an open-and-shut thing Chester was fated to get a terrible drubbing on that decisive day.

There were thousands on the field. Every seat in the grand-stand, as well as the commodious bleachers, was occupied, and countless numbers who would have willingly paid for a chance to take things comfortable, found it necessary to stand.

Chester had reason to feel proud of her awakening; and since it seemed an assured fact that her boys could do things worth while, there was reason to hope the town on Lake Constance would never again allow herself to sink back into her former condition of somnolence. So long as Jack Winters lived there, it might be understood first and last that such a catastrophe would never happen.

All eyes were upon the new pitcher who was yet to prove his worth. Most of those gathered to see the game only knew of Alec Donohue as a youngster who had been playing on the sand-lots, as that section near the factories was usually called, for there the toilers in the iron foundry and the mills were in the habit of playing scrub games.

Jack had come across Donohue by accident, and apparently must have been struck with the amazing speed and control that the boy showed in his delivery. He had taken Alec under his wing from that day on, and coached him, with the assistance of old Joe Hooker, until he felt confident he had picked up a real wonder.

Various comments were flying around, most of them connected with the newest member of the Chester team.

"One thing I like about that Donohue," a rangy scout of the high school was saying to a companion wearing glasses, and looking a bit effeminate, though evidently quite fond of sport; "he acts as though he might be as cool as a cucumber. Those Harmony fellows in the crowd will do their level best to faze him, if ever he gets in a tight corner, and lots of things are liable to happen through a hard-fought game."

"Oh! I asked Jack about that," observed the one with spectacles, "and he assured me the fellow seemed absolutely devoid of nerves. Nothing under the sun can bother him. He banks on Jack, and knows the captain has confidence in his work; so you'll see how all the jeering and whooping and stamping on the boards of the grand-stand will fail to upset him. Jack says he's an *iceberg*."

"Glad to hear it, Specs. That kind of pitcher always has a big lead over the fellow who gets excited as soon as the enemy begins to lambast his favorite curves. The cool sort just changes his gait, and lobs them over between, so that he has the hard batters wasting their energy on the air long before the ball gets across the rubber."

"Listen to all that whooping, Ernest; what's happening, do you think?"

"Well, by the way they're standing up on the seats, and waving hats and handkerchiefs, I rather guess the Harmony players are coming along."

His guess proved to be a true one, for a minute afterwards a big motor-stage entered the enclosure, and from it jumped a dozen or more athletic chaps clad in the spic-and-span white suits with blue stockings that distinguished the Harmony baseball team.

Paying little or no attention to all the wild clamor, they ran out on the near field and commenced flinging several balls back and forth with astonishing vigor. From time to time the boys from the rival town would wave a hand at some enthusiastic friend who was trying to catch their eye from his position in the stand, or on the bleachers.

The band had accompanied them aboard another vehicle. It now burst out with that same encouraging tune "Lo! the Conquering Hero Comes!" though the strains could hardly be heard above the roar of many lusty voices trying to drown each other out.

Of a truth, Chester had never seen such a wonderful day. It seemed as though the wand of a magician must have been manipulated to awaken the hitherto sleepy town to such real, throbbing life. And every boy in the place, yes, and girl also, not to mention hundreds of grown-ups who were thrilled with such a magnificent spectacle, had determined that this would only be a beginning; and that Chester must, under no conditions, be allowed to fall back into that old dead rut. Why, they had just begun to discover what living meant, and learn what the right sort of a spirit of sport will bring to a town.

It was now three, and after. The immense crowd began to grow impatient. Both teams had occupied the diamond in practice for fifteen minutes each, and many clever stunts were pulled off in clean pick-ups, and wonderful throws, which called forth bravos from the admiring spectators.

Several pitchers on either side had also warmed up, and naturally the new recruit, Donohue, was watched much more closely than those whose offerings had been seen on previous occasions.

He made no effort to disclose what he had in the way of various balls, his sole object, apparently, being to get his arm limbered up and in condition. Still, occasionally, he would send one in that caused a gasp to arise.

"Did you see that speed ball zip through the air, Specs?" demanded the fellow who had been called Ernest by the one wearing glasses.

"I tried to follow it, but lost out," admitted the other, frankly. "It's true, then, this Donohue must have a swift delivery, for I could always follow the ball when McGuffey hurled his best; and seldom lost one that speed-king Hendrix sent along. See how most of those Harmony chaps are looking out of the tail of their eyes at our man."

"They're trying to size Donohue up, that's all," said the knowing Ernest. "I've heard it said, though not able to vouch, for the truth of the rumor, that they've had a scout over in Chester every day for a week past."

"What for?" asked Specs.

"Trying to get a line on Donohue's delivery so as to report whether he's the wonder they've been told. But Jack was too clever for them, I guess. They say he had his battery off practicing in secret most of the while; and whenever Donohue did pitch for the local games he was held back. That's why some people said they believed he must be over-rated, and might prove a disappointment. But Jack only gave them the merry ha! ha! and told them to wait and see."

"But it's long after three right now, and still no sign of the game starting," continued Specs, a little anxiously.

"Yes," spoke up Oliver from his seat near by, "and, believe me, that bank of clouds looks a mite higher than it did when the Harmony fellows arrived. Unless they jig up right smart now, we'll get our jackets wet, you mark my words."

The others scoffed at his dismal prediction. With that bright sun shining up in the heavens, it did not seem possible that any such radical change in the weather could take place within a couple of hours.

"Hey! Big Bob, what's the matter with starting this game right away?" called Ernest, as the stalwart right-fielder of the local team chanced to be passing in the direction of the players' bench after chatting with friends.

"Umpire hasn't shown up yet!" called the accommodating Bob, raising his voice, as he knew hundreds were just as curious as Ernest concerning the mysterious reason for play not having commenced. "He had a break-down with his car on the way. Telephoned in that he would be half an hour late, and for them to get another umpire if they couldn't wait that long."

"Well, apparently, they've decided to wait," said Specs, resignedly, settling back in his seat for another fifteen minutes of listening to the chatter of a Babel of tongues and merry laughter. "Good umpires are almost as scarce as hens' teeth; and that Mr. Merrywether is reckoned as fair and impartial as they make them. So the game will start half an hour late after all!"

"Too bad!" Oliver was heard to say, with another apprehensive look in the direction of the southwest, as though to measure the location of that cloud bank with his weather-wise eye, and decide whether it gave promise of stopping play, perhaps at a most interesting stage of the game.

Most of those present did not begrudge the half hour thus spent. Just then none of them could even suspect how great an influence the lost time might have in respect to the eventual close of a fiercely contested game. But, as we shall see later on, it was fated that the dismal prophecies of Oliver were to have some foundation; and time cut a figure in the eventual outcome of that great day's rivalry on the diamond.

CHAPTER V
TIED IN THE NINTH INNING

The crowd stood up again, and there arose a jargon of cries followed by the appearance of a small wiry man dressed in blue, and wearing a cap after the usual type umpires prefer, so it seemed as though the delayed game would be quickly started.

When Hendrix, the expert hurler from Harmony, mowed down the first three men who faced him, two by way of vain strikes at his deceptive curves, and the other through a high foul, the shouts of the visitors told what an immense number of Harmony people had come across to see their favorites effectually stifle the rising ambition of Chester's athletes on the diamond.

Then came the turn of the locals in the field. Everything depended now on what Jack's new find could show in the way of pitching. Not an eye in that vast throng but was leveled at the youngster. It was certainly enough to try the nerve of any veteran, let alone a newcomer in the arena.

When his first ball sped across with a speed that made it fairly sizzle, many of the Chester rooters gave a shout of approval. Hutchings, the reliable first baseman of the visitors, had struck vainly at the ball. It was doubtful whether he had really seen it flash past, though it landed with a thud in Mullane's big mitt.

But the knowing ones from afar only laughed, and nodded their wise heads. They had seen speed before, and knew how often a pitcher "worked his arm off" in the start of a game, to fall a victim to their heavy batters later on. Unless this wonder of a youngster could stay with Hendrix through inning after inning, why, his finish could be seen. So they settled back in their seats with sighs of contentment, under the conviction that they might see a good game after all.

"Hendrix needs something to make him pitch his head off," remarked one of the visiting fans, in the hearing of Specs and Ernest. "He's taken things too easy most of the time. Why, not once this season so far has he been touched for as many hits as Chester got in the last game. It made the big fellow wake up, and we hear he's been doing a lot of practice lately. Today he ought to shine at his best."

"We all hope so, Mister," said Ernest, boldly, "because, unless the signs fail, he's going to need all his cunning this same day. That lad has the measure of your hard hitters already taken. Did you see him mow down Clifford then like a weed? Why, he'll have the best of them eating out of his hand before the day is done, believe me."

The gentleman only laughed. He could make allowances for a boy's natural enthusiasm. They did not know Hendrix at his best, as the Harmony folks did. He needed a little scare to force him to exert himself to the utmost. Yes, it really promised to be something of a game, if only the youngster kept going for half a dozen innings before he went to pieces, and the ball commenced to fly to every far corner of the field.

When the play was called the two nines on the diamond were lined up as follows:

Chester		Harmony
Jack Winters	*First Base*	Hatchings
Phil Parker	*Left Field*	Clifford
Herbert Jones	*Second Base*	Martin
Joel Jackman	*Centre Field*	Oldsmith
Toby Hopkins	*Shortstop*	Bailey
Big Bob Jeffries	*Right Field*	O'Leary
Fred Badger	*Third Base*	Young
Steve Mullane	*Catcher*	Chase
Alec Donohue	*Pitcher*	Hendrix

The first inning ended in no hits on either side. It looked very much as though the game might turn out to be a pitchers' duel. Some people like that sort of battle royal, but in the main the spectators would much rather see a regular old-fashioned batting fest, especially if it is *their* side that is doing most of the hitting.

Again did Hendrix start in to dazzle the locals with an exhibition of his wonderfully puzzling curves and drops. He certainly had them guessing, and in vain did they try to get the ball out of the diamond. Joel Jackman, the first man up, did manage to connect with the ball, perhaps by sheer accident. At the crack everybody held his or her breath and waited, for Joel was long-legged and a noted sprinter, so if only he got on first there might be some hope of succeeding batters working him around the circuit.

But Martin out near second made a leap, and snatched the ball off the ground as easily as though it were a habit of his to get anything that came within reach. He took his time to recover, and then sent the sphere to first as accurately as a bullet fired from a rifle.

Toby fouled three times, and then whiffed; while the swatter of the team, Big Bob, let a good one go by, and then vainly smote the air twice, for his judgment was certainly at fault, and the ball not where he thought it was.

Once again did Donohue step into the box, and after a few balls to Mullane, the first batter, Oldsmith, strode forward swinging his club, and looking especially dangerous. But when he only swung at the air, and backed away from the plate, shaking his head as though puzzled to know what it all meant, long and lusty yells broke out from the loyal Chester rooters.

Bailey, the alert little shortstop, managed to touch a whizzing ball, and send up a skyrocketing foul which Mullane amidst great excitement managed to get under, and smother in that big mitt of his.

Next in line came the terrible O'Leary. He was a swatter from away back, and all sorts of stories were circulated as to the number of home runs he had to his credit up to date.

Donohue looked perfectly cool and confident. He continued to send them in with a dazzling delivery. O'Leary allowed two to pass by, one strike being called on him by the alert umpire. Then he picked out a nice one, and there was an awful sound as he smote it with all his might and main.

Every one jumped up, and necks were stretched in the endeavor to follow the course of that wildly soaring ball, looking like a dot against the low sky-line.

"A homer!" shrieked scores of delighted Harmony fans.

"Watch Joel! He's after it!" shouted the local rooters, also thrilled by the spectacle of the long-legged centre fielder bounding over the ground like a "scared rabbit," as some of them said to themselves.

They saw Joel jump into the air and make a motion with his hand. Then he rolled over with a mighty lunge, but scrambled to his feet holding his hand aloft, to almost immediately hurl the ball in to Jones on second.

It had been a terrific swat, likewise a most amazing catch; and all of the yelling that burst forth was for Joel, who came trotting in, grinning happily, as though he rather liked that sort of thing.

And so the great game went on, inning after inning, amidst excitement that gripped every one present like a vise. When in the sixth Harmony managed to get a man on first through a fluke Texas leaguer, and began to work him along by bunt hitting, it looked dangerous for the locals. In the end, the visitors scored through a slip on the part of Herb Jones on second, who allowed the ball to get away from him because of his nervousness. The run was not earned, but it might decide the game, many people believed.

Jack put more ginger into his crowd when they went to bat in turn. The result of it was he himself made a neat single, and the crowd woke up to the fact that possibly Hendrix might not be so invincible as he was rated.

Up stepped Phil Parker with a grin, and pasted the sphere out in short left, advancing the runner a base with himself safely anchored on first. Jones did his duty and bunted, so that while he went out the runners were now on second and third with only one down.

It was amusing to see how the staid elderly men of Chester became excited at this critical juncture of the game. They could hardly keep their seats, and were watching the movements of those occupying the diamond as though the fate of nations depended on the outcome of this bitter rivalry in sport.

Joel Jackman was next. He, too, connected with the ball, but, alas, only to send up a tremendous foul that was promptly caught, after a smart run, by Clifford in short left field.

Everything depended on Toby Hopkins now. Toby was not known as a heavy hitter, but managed to connect frequently. He was due for a hit, the crowd yelled at him; whereupon the obliging Toby shot a swift one straight at Young on third. It was a hard ball to trap, and Young juggled it. Jack started like a blue streak for home as soon as he saw Toby had connected. He made a slide that carried him over the rubber just before Chase had the ball. It meant that the score was tied, with men on first and third, and two out.

Such shouts as broke forth, the very air seemed to quiver. Hope ran high as Bob Jeffries stepped up, swinging his bat. Alas! he failed miserably to connect with those puzzling curves of Hendrix, and after two vain strikes popped up a little infield fly to the pitcher that, of course, finished the exciting inning.

The game went on, without any more scoring until finally the ninth inning came. Both pitchers were doing as well or better than in the start, and it looked as though extra innings would be the rule. Such an outcome to a game always arouses great enthusiasm among the spectators. A few began to notice the fact that the sun was long since hidden by the rising clouds, and that overhead the blue had given place to a gray that looked suggestive of trouble.

Oliver in particular called attention to the fact that no matter how the other fellows had made fun of his prediction about the weather, it was likely to come true after all. If the game went into extra innings some of that mighty host of spectators might get soaking wet before they could find shelter.

Harmony was out to win the game in this inning. They had managed to get a line on Donohue's speed ball, or else guessed when it was coming over, for the first man up, Clifford, got a safety past short that Toby only stopped by such an effort that he rolled over, and by the time he could deliver the ball to Jack the runner had gone leaping past the bag and was safe.

Pandemonium broke loose just then. The Harmony crowd yelled and whooped and carried on as though a legion of real lunatics had broken out of an asylum near by.

"Here's where we clinch the game, Chester!"

"It's all over!"

"Martin, your turn to swat the bean!"

"Get Donohue going at last. The best pitcher may go to the wall once too often, especially the Harmony well!"

"Now make it three this inning, boys, and we'll forgive you for holding back all this time!"

These and dozens of other cries could be heard. They were partly intended to flustrate the Chester slab-artist, and make him send in the ball wildly, so that the next man might be given his base, something that had only occurred once thus far with Donohue. But Jack sent him a cheering word, and Donohue seemed as cool as ice as he proceeded to serve Captain Martin with his choice swift ones.

CHAPTER VI
FRED PUT TO THE TEST

Through the game, Jack had been observing just how Fred Badger carried himself. Since hits were so few and far between thus far, he had not had a great deal to do in the field. Once he ran in on a bunt, and got it to first in time to cut off the runner. No one could have carried out the play in better shape. Another time he took a hot liner straight off the bat, and received a salvo of cheers from the crowd, always pleased to see such clever play, no matter on which side it occurs.

At bat Fred had not succeeded in shining brilliantly. Hendrix was apparently a puzzle to him, as to many another player. He struck out twice, and perished on a foul another time; but there could be no doubt Fred was trying his best to get in a drive that might be effectual.

Jack noticed that he often cast glances in the direction of the grandstand where a number of enthusiastic Chester girls sat, and waved their flags or handkerchiefs whenever anything occurred that aroused their admiration. He remembered that pretty Molly Skinner was seated there. Fred evidently had not forgotten that fact either, and Jack found himself hoping it might have considerable influence with the sorely tempted third baseman, in case he were finally put to the test.

Martin was apparently out for a hit, if one could judge from his determined attitude as he stood there at the plate, and swung his bat back and forth in his own peculiar fashion, meanwhile watching the pitcher like a hawk.

The coaching had become vehement, Harmony players seeking to unnerve Donohue by running back and forth around first, until the umpire called a halt on this proceeding, after Jack had drawn his attention to the infringement of the rules.

Then Martin swung. He missed connection, and a groan arose from his crowd, while the Chester contingent cheered Donohue lustily. But Martin only smiled. Such a little thing as that was not going to faze him. He had still two more chances, and the next time he would make more certain.

A deathly silence fell upon the crowd, waiting to see whether Harmony could pull the game out of the fire in the ninth, as had happened several times that same season, for they were famous on account of their rallies.

Martin had a second strike called on him, though he made no effort to go after the ball. In fact, it must have passed him so speedily that he could not properly gauge whether it would be a strike or a ball.

Then suddenly Donohue, taking his cue from a motion Jack made, changed his pace. Although he went through exactly the same gyrations as though about to send up another swift one, the ball came lazily floating through the air, and Martin was seen to viciously stab with his bat long before there was any chance to make connections.

Bedlam broke loose again at that. Auto horns and sirens tooted strenuously, boys shrieked through megaphones, girls waved their flags furiously, and Donohue was greeted with encouraging shouts from every side. Really, he was working wonderfully well considering that he could be called a newcomer to the diamond. In time he was certain to make a name for himself among the big clubs, if some wandering scout ever heard of him, and visited Chester to size his work up.

But here came Oldsmith, and there was that about his manner to proclaim how his whole heart was bent on making at least a single, if not better, so that Harmony might break the tie, and get the home team on the run.

"Take him into camp, Alec!"

"You've got his measure all right, old scout! Twice before he whiffed, and he's in line to make it three times!"

"Feed him your best sizzlers, Donohue!"

"Oldsmith, you're a back number today, don't you know?"

Then they heard the bat connect with the ball. Clifford was off toward second in great style. Toby Hopkins threw himself and managed to stop the shoot that was headed for centre, but he could not get to Jones on second in time to nail the runner, for the umpire held up his hand, and that meant Clifford was safe.

Again things began to look dark for Chester. Harmony had "found" Donohue at last, it seemed, and there could be no telling when the salvo of hits could stop. Perhaps the game would be "sewed up" right there, in case Harmony scored, and Hendrix shut his opponents out when their turn at bat came.

Now it was Bailey up.

The little shortstop was primed for anything. He struck at the first ball, and knocked a foul which dropped safe. Then he missed the next ball so that he was "two in the hole." Of course it was expected that Donohue would now try to deceive him by tempting him with a curve that would be wide of the plate; but Jack had signaled for a third one straight, and it came with swiftness.

Bailey was ready, however, and knew he had to strike, for it would count against him at any rate. He got a fluke hit that started toward first. By jumping in Jack managed to pick up the ball, and then having touched the bag, he hurled it toward second in hopes of making a double play.

Oldsmith, however, had made a fine slide, and was clutching the corner of the second sack when Jones took the ball; while Clifford had won third.

There were now two down, with men on second and third.

Everything depended on the next batter, and when it was seen to be that formidable slugger O'Leary, the home-run maker, how those Harmony rooters did scream. Some of the more irresponsible took to dancing like idiots, clasped in each other's arms. In fact, every known device for "rattling" a pitcher was resorted to, of course legitimately, in order to further their waning cause.

Eagerly did many of the local fans watch to see whether Donohue gave any evidence of going to pieces. He seemed as cool as ever, and smiled as he handled the ball; while O'Leary was knocking his big bat on the ground to test its reliability, as though he meant to put it to some good service then and there. He was seen to turn his head and grin toward some of his ardent admirers in the bleachers back of him. By this means he doubtless informed them that he had been only playing with the tenderfoot pitcher hitherto, and would now proceed to show what strength lay in those muscular arms of his.

Jack waved the fielders back. He anticipated that O'Leary was due for one of his famous lengthy drives, and it was necessary that those guarding the outer gardens should be in position to make a great run, once the ball left the bat. Still, he continued to feel fairly confident that Donohue would recover from his temporary set-back, and possibly deceive O'Leary, as he had done twice before.

He realized that the crisis he had feared was now upon them. If O'Leary sent a scorcher toward Fred, how would the third baseman handle it? Clifford knew what was expected of him, and already part way home on the movement of the pitcher winding up to throw, he would shoot along at the crack of the bat, taking his chances, since there were already two down.

He saw O'Leary actually turn his head slightly and take a quick look toward third as though making up his mind just where he wanted to send the ball, should he be able to connect with the horse-hide sphere. Jack felt a cold chill pass over him. Could it be possible that O'Leary actually *knew* there was a weak link in the chain made by the infield, and figured on taking advantage of Fred's intended treachery?

At that moment it seemed as though Jack lived years, so many things flashed into his mind. He even remembered how earlier in the game two men, strangers in town, had made themselves obnoxious by standing up in the bleacher seats and shaking handfuls of greenbacks, daring Chester people to back their favorites at odds of three to four. They had been spotted almost immediately, and the mayor of Chester ordered them to desist under penalty of being arrested, since it was against the law of the town for any sort of wagering to be indulged in.

The presence of the local police, and their movement toward the spot had resulted in the two sporty looking strangers subsiding. Some of the Harmony boys, however, scoffed at such Puritanical methods of procedure, since over at their town things were allowed to run wide open; or at least winked at by the authorities.

Jack had been too far away to make sure, but he had a suspicion that one of the pair of betting men looked very much like the party with whom he had seen Fred Badger in close conversation, and who had offered him a paper to sign, after which something passed between them that might have been money, though Jack had not been absolutely certain about that part of it.

Deep down in his heart, Jack hoped most earnestly that the chance for Fred to soil his hands with any crooked work might not arise. It would be all right, for instance, if only Donohue could strike the great O'Leary out for the third time. Then again perhaps even though the batter managed to connect with the ball, he might be unable to send it straight toward Fred. It was liable to go in any other direction, and if a tally should result from the blow, at least it could not be placed to a supposed error on the part of Badger.

Donohue delivered his first one wide of the plate. O'Leary laughed, and nodded his head, as though to tell the pitcher he was too old a bird to be caught with such chaff.

"Make him put it over, Dan!"

"Knock the stuffing out of the ball, O'Leary!"

"One of your old-time homers is what we need, remember!"

"You've got his number, Dan; don't bite at a wide one!"

"You'll walk, all right; he's afraid of you, old scout!"

All these and many other cries could be heard, but the players were paying no attention to the crowd now. Every fielder was "on his toes," so to speak, anticipating that it might be up to him to save the day. In the main, the crowd was so anxious over the outcome of the next ball from the pitcher that they almost forgot to breathe, only watching the pitcher wind up preparatory to making his throw.

Jack saw Fred give one of his quick looks toward the spot where pretty Molly Skinner sat. He hoped it meant that he had resolved to be staunch and true to his team-mates, and loyal to his native town, despite any terrible temptation that may have come to him in the shape of a big bribe.

O'Leary had a peculiar crouch at the plate. His odd attitude made Jack think of a squatty spider about to launch itself at a blue-bottled fly that had ventured too near his corner. No doubt it accounted in some measure for his swatting ability, as he would necessarily put the whole force of his body in his blow. Often when he missed connections he would whirl all the way around; and then recovering make a humorous gesture toward his admirers in the crowd, for O'Leary, being Irish, was almost always in good humor, no matter what happened.

He let the first ball speed past for a strike, and higher rose the excitement. The umpire called the second one a ball, which evened matters a little. Next came "strike two," and yet the great O'Leary waited, while his admirers began to feel fainthearted, fearing that he would stand there and be counted down when everything depended on his making a hit.

Then there came an awful crack! O'Leary had picked out just the kind of a ball he wanted. It must have left his bat like a bullet, and Jack felt himself turn cold when he realized that the ball was headed straight as a die for Fred Badger!

CHAPTER VII
THE GAME CALLED BY DARKNESS

A terrible roar broke forth from thousands of throats. Jack had actually closed his eyes for just a second, unable to witness what might be a plain palpable muff on the part of the tempted Fred. As he opened them again, unmindful of the fact that the batter was rushing toward him with all possible speed, he saw that while Fred had knocked the ball down he had also made a quick recovery.

Just then, he was in the act of hurling it toward home, where Mullane had braced himself to receive the throw, and tag the oncoming runner out. Should Fred veer ever so little from a direct line throw he would pull the catcher aside, and thus give Clifford the opportunity he wanted to slide home.

Away went the ball. Jack held his breath. He saw Mullane, reliable old Mullane, make a quick movement with his hands, and then throwing himself forward, actually fall upon the prostrate and sliding form of the Harmony lad.

"You're out!"

That was the umpire making his decision. Not one of the Harmony fellows as much as lifted a voice to dispute the verdict; in the first place, they knew Mr. Merrywether too well to attempt browbeating him at the risk of being taken out of the game; then again every one with eyes could see that Clifford had been three feet away from the plate when Mullane tagged him with the ball.

How the crowd did carry on. A stranger chancing on the spot might have thought Pershing's gallant little army had managed to capture the Kaiser, or crossed the Rhine on its way to Berlin. Indeed, those "whoopers" could not have made more noise to the square inch under any conditions.

And Jack's one thought was gratitude that after all Fred had been able to come through the great test with his honor unsullied. He had shot the ball as straight as a die at Mullane; and the game was still anybody's so far as victory was concerned.

They played a tenth inning, and still not a runner so much as reached second. Really both pitchers seemed to be getting constantly better, strange to say, for they mowed the batters down in succession, or else caused them to pop up fouls that were readily captured by the first or third basemen, or the man behind the bat.

This was not so wonderful on the part of the veteran Hendrix, for he was well seasoned in the game, and had been known to figure in a thirteen-inning deal, coming out ahead in the end when his opponent weakened. Everybody, however, declared it to be simply marvelous that a greenhorn slab-artist like young Donohue should prove to be the possessor of so much stamina.

The eleventh inning went through in quick order. Still the tie remained unbroken, though Jack managed to get a single in his turn at bat. Phil Parker also rapped a ferocious screamer across the infield, but hit into a double that ended the hopeful rally at bat.

When the twelfth opened up, a number of people were seen to start away. They may have been enthusiastic fans enough, but the day was waning, home might be far distant, and they did not like the way those clouds had rolled up, promising a storm sooner or later.

The sun was out of sight long since, and objects could not be determined as easily as when the game began. Every little while that weather-sharp, Oliver, would take a sailor-like squint aloft, and chuckle to himself. Indeed, Specs, his companion, was of the opinion that Oliver would be willing to cheerfully take a good ducking if he could only have his scorned prediction prove a true shot.

There were those present so intent on the game that they paid no attention to the gathering clouds, and the fact that it was getting difficult to see the ball. This latter fact was depended on to help bring matters to a focus, because errors were more likely to occur, any one of which might prove sufficient to let in the winning run.

But if the fielders were thus handicapped, the batters had their own troubles. They could not distinguish the fast-speeding ball as it shot by, and consequently were apt to whack away at anything, so strike-outs must become the order of the day.

The twelfth ended with nothing doing on either side. By now some of the boys were beginning to tire out, for the long strain was telling on them. These fellows of weak hearts were willing to have the game called a draw, which must be played over again at Harmony on the succeeding Saturday. As playing on the home ground is usually considered a great advantage, because the players are accustomed to every peculiarity of the field, Harmony would reap more or less profit from having the postponed game on their diamond. And consequently, when they trooped out for the finish of the thirteenth inning, several of them seemed to have conspired to delay play as much as possible.

This they did in various ways. One fellow made out to have received a slight injury, and the umpire called time until a companion could wrap a rag around the scratched finger. Doubtless he would hardly like to show the extent of his hurt, but the wide grin on his face after the tedious operation had been concluded, told the truth; indeed, most of those present were able to guess his object.

Then just as they settled down to play, another fielder called for time while he knelt down to fasten his shoe-lace which seemed to have come undone, and might trip him at a critical time when he was racing for a fly.

The crowd yelled and jeered, but in spite of all, Clifford took a full minute and more to effect his purpose. Finally, rising, he waved his hand to the umpire to let him know the game could now proceed.

The crowd knew that Harmony was fighting for time, anxious now to have the game called a draw, so that they might have another chance on their home grounds. Such yelling as took place. Harmony was loudly accused of weakening, and trying to crawl out of a tight hole. Loud calls were made for Big Bob at bat to knock one over the fence and lose the ball for keeps.

He did his best, and every one leaped up when the sound of his bat striking the pellet sounded above all other noises. The ball went screeching over second, and apparently was tagged for a three-bagger at least; but Oldsmith had been playing deep when he saw who was up, and by making a most desperate effort he managed to clutch the ball just in time.

That was the expiring effort on the part of Chester. The other two batters went out in quick order just as the first few drops of rain started to fall.

It was now getting quite gloomy, and a hurried consultation between the umpire and the rival captains resulted in Mr. Merrywether announcing through a megaphone that the game would have to be declared a draw, which tie must be played off at Harmony, according to previous arrangements, on the following Saturday.

Then the vast crowd commenced to scatter in a great hurry, fearful lest the rain start falling and drench them. There was more or less confusion as scores of cars and carryalls rushed along the road leading to Harmony, distant ten miles or more. Since everybody hurried, the grounds were soon deserted save by a few who remained to look after things.

Jack and several of the boys would have lingered to talk matters over, but the lateness of the hour and the overcast sky forbade such a thing, so they, too, headed for their various homes.

Jack, however, did manage to locate Fred, and made it a point to overtake the other on the road. He linked his arm with that of the third baseman, and dropped into step.

"I want to say, Fred, that stop and throw of yours saved the day for Chester," he told the other. "If you had drawn Steve a foot away from home Clifford would have slid safe, for he was coming like a hurricane. Chester will remember that fine work of yours for a long time. And the girls, Fred, why I thought they'd have a fit, they carried on so. I'm sure you pleased some of your best friends a whole lot by being Johnny-on-the-spot today!"

"Thank you for saying it, anyhow, Jack," the other was saying, and somehow Jack could not help thinking Fred did not show just as much gratification as most fellows would have done at being so highly complimented.

But then, he must make allowances. If matters were as desperate as he suspected, poor Fred must by now be feeling the effect of having allowed his chance for securing all that money, so badly needed in order to help his mother, slip through his fingers. Now that all the excitement had died away, and he found himself face to face with the old question, with the prospect of seeing his mother's tired looks again reproaching him, Fred must be wondering whether he had after all chosen wisely in letting honor take the place of duty.

So Jack commenced to chatter about the game, and how proud Chester folks would be of the young athletes who represented the town that day.

"It's pretty evident, you must see, Fred," he continued, after thus arousing the other's interest, "that our big task of getting subscriptions toward building or renting a building for a club-house and gymnasium has been helped mightily by the clever work done this day. I heard of three influential gentlemen who had declared they were willing to take a hand, just because such determined and hard-playing boys stood in need of such an institution."

"Yes, Chester has been away behind the times in looking after the morals and requirements of her young people," admitted Fred. "There's Marshall with its fine Y. M. C. A. building and gym., and even Harmony has a pretty good institution where the young fellows can belong, and spend many a winter's evening in athletic stunts calculated to build up their bodies, and make them more healthy."

"Well, believe me, the day is about to dawn when Chester will be put on the map for the same stuff," asserted Jack, not boastingly, but with full confidence; "and these splendid baseball matches we're pulling off nowadays are bound to help to bring that same event to pass. Men who had almost forgotten that they used to handle a bat in their kid days have had their old enthusiasm for the national sport of America revived. Depend upon it, Fred, in good time we'll be playing football, hockey, basketball, and every sort of thing that goes to make up the life of a healthy boy."

In this fashion did the pair talk as they hurried along. The drops were beginning to come down faster now, showing that when the game was called, it had been a very wise move, for many people must otherwise have been caught in the rain.

Fred seemed to be fairly cheerful at the time Jack shook his hand again, and once more congratulated him on his fine work for the team. Looking back after they had parted, Jack saw the boy stop at his door and hesitate about entering, which seemed to be a strange thing for a member of the gallant baseball team that had covered themselves with glory on that particular day to do.

But then Jack could guess how possibly Fred might be feeling his heart reproach him again because he had chosen his course along the line of honor. He must get a grip on himself before he could pass in and see that weary look on her face. Jack shook his head as he hurried on to his own house. He felt that possibly the crisis in Fred's young life had, after all, only been postponed, and not altogether passed. That terrible temptation might come to him again, more powerful than ever; and in the game at Harmony, if a choice were given him, would he be just as able to resist selling himself as he had on this wonderful day?

CHAPTER VIII
THE PUZZLE GROWS

It was just three days afterwards when Jack saw his two chums again. On Sunday morning his father had occasion to start to a town about thirty miles distant, to see a sick aunt who depended on him for advice. She had sent word that he must fetch Jack along with him, Jack being the old lady's special favorite and probably heir to her property.

Jack's father was a lawyer, and often had trips to make in connection with real estate deals, and estates that were located in distant parts. Consequently, it was nothing unusual for him to receive a sudden call. Jack might have preferred staying in Chester, where things were commencing to grow pretty warm along the line of athletics, his favorite diversion. His parents, however, believed it would be unwise to offend the querulous old dame who was so crotchetty that she might take it into her head to change her will, and leave everything to some society for the amelioration of the condition of stray cats. It would be a great pity to have all that fine property go out of the Winters' family, they figured; and perhaps they were wise in thinking that way; little Jack cared about it, not being of a worldly mind.

So when he sighted Toby and Steve on the afternoon of his return, he gave the pair a hail, and quickly joined them on the street.

"Glad you've got back home, Jack, sure I am," said Toby, the first thing.

"Why," added Steve, "we didn't even get a chance to compare notes with you about that great game on Saturday, though Toby and myself have talked the subject threadbare by now."

"And one thing we both agree about, Jack," continued Toby, with a grin.

"What's that?" demanded the other.

"Fred saved the day when he stopped that terrible line drive of O'Leary, and shot the ball home as straight as a die. No professional player could possibly have done it a shade better, I'm telling you."

"It was a grand play," admitted Jack, "and I told Fred so while we walked home together."

Steve looked keenly at him when Jack said this.

"Oh! then you got a chance to talk with Fred after the game, did you?" he ventured to say, in a queer sort of way. "How did Fred act then, Jack?"

"Well, I must say he didn't impress me as being over-enthusiastic," admitted Jack. "You see, he had done his whole duty in the heat of action, and after he had a chance to cool off and realize what he had lost, he may have felt a touch of remorse, for he certainly does love that poor mother of his a heap. I can understand just how he must be having a terrible struggle in his mind as to what is the right course for him to pursue."

At that Toby gave a snort that plainly told how he was beginning to doubt certain things in which he had hitherto fully believed.

"Now, looky here, Jack," he started to say good-humoredly, "don't you reckon that you might have been mistaken in thinking poor Fred was dickering with some of those men to throw the game, so they could make big money out of if? Why, after all, perhaps his looking so dismal comes from his feeling so bad about his mother. We ought to give him the benefit of the doubt, I say."

"I sometimes feel that way myself, Toby, don't you know?" acknowledged Jack in his usual frank fashion. "And yet when I consider the conditions, and remember how suspiciously Fred acted with that sporty-looking gentleman, I find myself owning up that it looks bad for the boy. But at any rate he succeeded in fighting his own battle, and winning a victory over his temptation."

"But, Jack, I'm afraid he's bound to have to go through the whole business again," interposed Steve.

"Do you know I more than half suspected you had got wind of something new in the affair, Steve," Jack told him. "I could see how your eyes glistened as you listened to what Toby here was saying; and once or twice you opened your mouth to interrupt him, but thought better of it. Now tell us what it means, Steve."

"For one thing, that man has been at Fred again," asserted the other, positively.

"Do you know this for a certainty?" Jack asked.

"Why, I saw them talking, I tell you," explained Steve, persistently. "This is how it came about. You see, yesterday, as Toby here couldn't go fishing with me I started off alone, taking my bait pail and rod along, and bent on getting a mess of perch at a favorite old fishin' hole I knew along the shore of the lake about a mile or so from town."

"Meaning that same place you showed me, near where the road comes down close to the shore of the water?" suggested Toby, quickly.

"Right you are, son," continued Steve, nodding his head as he spoke. "Well, I had pretty fair luck for a while, and then the perch quit taking hold, so I sat down to wait till they got hungry again. And while I squatted there on the log that runs out over the water at my favorite hole, I heard the mutter of voices as some people came slowly along the road.

"First I didn't pay much attention to the sounds, believing that just as like as not it was a couple of town boys, and I didn't like the idea of their finding out where I got such heavy strings of fish once in so often. And then as they passed closer to me something familiar in one of the voices made me twist my head around.

"Well, it was Fred Badger, all right, walking along with that same sporty-looking stranger. And say, he isn't such a bad-looking customer after all, Jack, when you get a close look at him, being gray-bearded, and a bit halting in his walk like he might have been injured some time or other. It's more the clothes he wears that give him the sporty appearance, though, if you say he's one of that betting bunch up at Harmony, he must be a bad lot.

"They had their heads together, and seemed to be discussing something at a great rate. I couldn't hear what they said, the more the pity, for it might have given us a line on the whole silly business; but the man seemed trying to convince Fred about something, and the boy was arguing kind of feebly as if ready to give in. Well, something tempted me to give a cough after I'd stood up on the log. Both of 'em looked that way in a hurry. I waved my hand at Fred, and he answered my signal, but while you might have expected that he'd come back to ask what luck I had, and mebbe introduce his friend, he didn't do that same by a jugfull. Fact is he said something to the man, and the two of them hurried along the road."

Jack felt his heart grow heavy again. He was taking a great interest in the affairs of Fred Badger, and would be very much shocked should the other fall headlong into the net that seemed to be spread for his young feet.

"I know for one thing," he told the others, "I'll be mighty glad when that tie game is played off with Harmony, no matter which side wins the verdict. And I hope Fred is given no such chance to choose between right and wrong as came his way last Saturday. If those men increase the bribe his scruples may give way. And if only Fred could understand that his mother would utterly refuse to profit by his dishonor, he might have his heart steeled to turn the tempters down."

"Then, Jack, why don't you try and figure out how you could put it up to Fred that way?" urged Toby, eagerly.

"I've tried to think how it could be done without offending him, or allowing him to suspect that I know what he's going through," mused Jack. "There might be a way to mention a hypothetical case, as though it were some other fellow I once knew who had the same kind of choice put up to him, and took the wrong end, only to have his father or sister, for whom he had sinned, reproach him bitterly, and refuse to accept tainted money."

"Gee whiz! it does take you to hatch up ways and means, Jack!" exclaimed Toby, delightedly. "Now, I should say that might be a clever stunt. You can warn him without making him feel that you're on to his game. Figure it out, Jack, and get busy before next Saturday comes, won't you?"

"Yes," added Steve, "Fred Badger is too good a fellow to let drop. We need him the worst kind to fill that gap at third. Besides, suspecting what we do, it would be a shame for us not to hold out a helping hand to a comrade who's up against it good and hard."

"What you say, Steve, does your big heart credit," remarked Jack, "but it might be wise for us to drop our voices a little, because somehow we have wandered on, and are right now getting pretty close to Fred's home, which you know lies just on the other side of that clump of bushes."

"Did you steer us this way on purpose, Jack!" demanded Toby, suspiciously.

"Why, perhaps I had a little notion of stopping in and seeing Mrs. Badger," admitted the other, chuckling. "In fact, my mother commissioned me to fetch this glass of home-made preserves over to her, knowing that Fred's mother has not been at all well. Yes, I own up I was influential in making her think that way, and was on my way when I ran across you fellows."

"Huh! I wouldn't be at all surprised, Jack!" declared Toby, "if you had a scheme in your mind right now to put a crimp in this foolishness on the part of Fred Badger."

"I'm not saying I haven't, remember, fellows," laughed the other, who evidently did not mean to show his full hand just then. "When the time comes perhaps I'll let you in on this thing. I want to do some more thinking first, though. Many a good idea is wasted because it isn't given a foundation in the beginning. Now, suppose you boys wait for me here while I step around and leave this little comfit with Mrs. Badger with my mother's compliments."

"Just as you say, Jack," muttered Steve, looking rather unhappy because lie was not to be taken wholly into the confidence of the other. "Don't stay too long, though, unless you mean to tell us all that happens in there."

Jack only smiled in return, and stepped forward. His comrades saw him suddenly draw back as though he had made a discovery. Then turning toward them, he beckoned with his hand, at the same time holding up a warning finger as though telling them not to make the least noise.

"Now, what's in the wind, Jack?" whispered Toby, as they reached the side of the other.

"Take a peek and see who's here!" Jack told them.

At that both the others advanced cautiously and stared beyond the big clump of high bushes. They almost immediately shrank back again, and the look on their faces announced the receipt of quite a shock.

"Great Cæsar! is that chap the man you've both been talking about, tell me?" asked Toby, half under his breath.

"He is certainly the party I saw Fred talking with so mysteriously," asserted Jack, positively.

"And the same fellow who was walking along the road with Fred while I sat on my log, fishing," added Steve, convincingly.

"But what under the sun is he doing out here near Fred's house, leaning on that fence, and keeping tabs on the little Badger home, I'd like to know?" Toby went on to say, wonder written in big letters on his face.

CHAPTER IX
A FAIRY IN THE BADGER HOME

"Let's watch and see what it all means?" suggested Steve, quickly.

Even Jack did not seem averse to doing that same thing. In fact, his curiosity had been aroused to fever pitch by so unexpectedly discovering the very man of whom they had been lately talking hovering around poor Fred's home in such a suspicious fashion.

Peeping around the high bushes again, they saw him leaning idly on the picket fence. He seemed to have a stout cane, and was smoking a cigar, though in his undoubted eagerness to keep "tabs" on the humble house he forgot to draw smoke from the weed between his teeth.

"I must say this is going it pretty strong," grumbled Toby, half under his breath; "to have that chap prowling around Fred's home, just like he was afraid the boy'd get out of his grip, and so meant to find a stronger hold on him."

"That's it," assented Steve; "he wants to learn why Fred seems to hold back. He means to meet the little mother, and the two small girls, one of 'em a cripple in the bargain. It's a shame that he should push himself in on that family, and he a city sport in the bargain. We ought to find a way to chase him out of town, don't you think, Jack?"

"Hold up, and perhaps we may learn something right now," whispered the other, after a hasty look; "because there's Fred's mother coming out of the door."

"Gee whiz! can she be meaning to meet this man?" ventured Toby, apparently appalled by his own suspicion.

"Well, hardly likely," Jack told him, "because the man has ducked down as if he didn't want to be seen by her, though he's looking like everything all the while."

"That's little Barbara Badger, the five-year-old sister of Fred," Steve was saying. "She's got a basket on her arm, too, and I reckon her ma is sending her to the store down the street for a loaf of bread, or something like that. Everybody seems to agree that Barbara is the most winsome little girl in the whole of Chester."

"Barring none," admitted Toby, immediately. "Why, she's just like a little golden-haired fairy, my dad says, and since he's something of an artist he ought to know when he sees one. Yep, you were right,

Steve, the child is going after something at the store. I wonder now would that wretch have the nerve to stop Barbara, and try to get some information from the little thing?"

"What if he tries to kidnap her?" suggested Steve, suddenly, doubling up his sturdy looking fist aggressively, as though to indicate that it would not be safe for the stranger to attempt such a terrible thing while he was within hearing distance.

"Oh! I hardly think there's any fear of that happening," Jack assured the aggressive member of the trio. "But he acts now as if he meant to drop back here out of sight, so perhaps we'd better slip around this bunch of bushes so he won't learn how we've been watching him."

Suiting their actions to Jack's words, the three boys quickly "made themselves scarce," which was no great task when such an admirable hiding-place as that stack of bushes lay conveniently near by. Sure enough, the stranger almost immediately came around the clump and made sure that it hid him from the small cottage lying beyond. Jack, taking a look on his own account from behind the bushes, saw that Mrs. Badger had started to reenter the house; while pretty little Barbara was contentedly trudging along the cinder pavement.

Evidently the child was quite accustomed to doing errands of this nature for her mother, when Fred did not happen to be around; nor was it likely that Mrs. Badger once dreamed Barbara might get into any sort of trouble, for the neighborhood, while not fashionable, was at least said to be safe, and honest people dwelt there.

"He's staring as hard as anything at Barbara," whispered Toby, who had been peeping. "Why, he acts for all the world like he could fairly eat the sweet little thing up. Perhaps it's a good job we chance to be around here after all," but Jack shook his head as though he did not dream any harm was going to come to little Barbara.

"If he's so much taken up watching her," he remarked, "we can spy on him without his being any the wiser. But take care not to move too quickly at any time; and a sneeze or a cough would spoil everything for us."

Accordingly, they crept forward. Looking cautiously around their covert, the boys could easily see that Barbara Badger had by now turned the bushes and reached the spot where the stranger stood.

Now he was speaking to her, bending low, and using what struck the suspicious Steve as a wheedling tone; though to Jack it was just what any gentleman might use in seeking to gain the confidence of a child who had never seen him before.

Apparently the little girl did not seem to be afraid. Perhaps she was accustomed to having people speak kindly to her on the street, just to see that winsome smile break over her wonderfully pretty face. At any rate, she had answered him, and as he started to walk slowly at her side, it seemed as though they had entered into quite an animated conversation, the stranger asking questions, and the little girl giving such information as lay in her power.

"He's just trying to find out how the land lies in Fred's house, that's what he's doing, the sneak!" gritted Steve.

"Oh! how do we know but what the man has a small girl of his own somewhere?" Jack interposed; "and Barbara somehow reminds him of her. Besides, can you blame anybody for trying to get acquainted with Fred's sweet little sister?"

Steve subsided after that. Apparently he could find no answer to the logic Jack was able to bring against his suspicions. By skirting the inside of a fence it would be possible for them to follow after the man and the child without disclosing their presence.

"Let's do it!" suggested Steve, after Toby had made mention of this fact.

Accordingly they started to steal along. As the others were walking very slowly the three boys found no great difficulty in keeping close behind them. They could even pick up something of what passed between the pair on the cinder pavement. The man was asking Barbara about her home folks, and seemed particularly interested in hearing about mother's pale looks and many sighs; and also how sister Lucy seemed to be able to walk better lately than at any time in the past; though she did have to use a crutch; but she hoped to be able to go to school in the fall if she continued to improve.

Fred's name did not seem to be mentioned once by the man. Even when Barbara told some little thing in which the boy figured, the man failed to ask about him. His whole interest was centered in the mother, the crippled child, and this wonderfully attractive little angel at his side.

Jack also noticed that he had hold of Barbara's small hand, which he seemed to be clutching eagerly. Yes, it must be the man had a daughter of his own far away, and memories of her might be making him sorry that he had engaged in such a disreputable business as tempting Barbara's brother to betray his mates of the baseball team.

Then the man stopped short. He had looked around and discovered that if he went any further he might be noticed from the side windows of the Badger cottage. Apparently he did not wish that the child's mother should discover him walking with her. Jack somehow felt an odd thrill shoot through him when he saw the man suddenly bend his head and press several kisses on the little hand that had been nestling so confidingly in his own palm. That one act seemed to settle it in the boy's mind that there was more or less truth in his conjecture in connection with another Barbara in some distant city waiting for her father to come back home.

"Say, he's acting real spoony, isn't he, Jack?" gasped Toby, taken aback as he saw the man do this. "I reckon now, Steve, your ogre isn't *quite* as tough a character as you imagined. He's got a spark of human about him, seems like, and like most Chester folks has to knuckle down before that pretty kid."

"Oh! he may be acting that way for a purpose," grumbled the unconvinced Steve, still unwilling to give up. "Such fellows generally have a deep game up their sleeve, you understand. Just wait and see, that's all, Toby Hopkins. I don't like his actions one little bit, if you want to know how I feel about it."

Almost immediately afterwards Toby spoke again in a guarded tone.

"Look at her picking something up from among the cinders, and holding it out! Why, it looks like a shining new fifty-cent bit, which is just what it is. And to think we walked right over it when we came along, and not one of us glimpsed what the sharp eyes of that child have found."

"Huh! mebbe it wasn't there when we came along, Toby!" suggested Steve. "Just as like as not that chap he dropped the coin, and ground it part-way into the cinders with his toe, then managed so little Barbara should pick it up. There, listen to him now telling her that findings is keepings, and that the money belongs to her by right of discovery. That was a smart dodge, wasn't it? I wonder what his game is. Can you guess it, Jack?"

"I decline to commit myself to an answer," came the reply.

"That means you've got some sort of hazy suspicion, which may and again may not pan out later on," hinted Steve. "Oh! well, it seems as if we've run smack up against a great puzzle, and I never was a good hand at figuring such things out—never guessed a rebus or an acrostic in my whole life. Tell us when you strike pay dirt, that's a good fellow, Jack."

"Perhaps I will," chuckled the other, still keeping his eyes glued on the figures of little Barbara and the stranger, not far distant.

Now the man had evidently said good-bye, for, as she tripped along the walk, she turned to wave her chubby hand to him, and even kiss the tips of her fingers to her scarlet rosebud lips as if sending a kiss back.

He stood there staring after her. Jack watching saw him take out a handkerchief and wipe his eyes several times. Apparently that meeting with Barbara Badger had affected the man considerably. Jack hoped it would be for his good, and also for the benefit of Fred Badger, who seemed to be struggling with some secret that was weighing his young spirit down.

Then the man turned and looked long and earnestly back toward the humble cottage home of the widow. He was shaking his head and muttering something half under his breath; but somehow Jack thought he did not look very ferocious just then. In fact, after the man strode away and they were free to once more come out on the walk, Jack had a feeling that the stranger did not appear quite so much like a desperate city sport as he had formerly believed.

CHAPTER X
THE WARNING

"Hello! there, Jack, you're wanted!"

The boys were practicing on the following afternoon when this hail reached the ears of the first baseman, diligently stopping terrific grounders that came from the bat of substitute catcher, Hemming, the best man on the nine for this sort of work.

So Jack trotted in toward the group near the bench. A score or two of boys, with also a sprinkling of enthusiastic girls, had gathered to watch and admire the different plays which were put through, and to generously applaud any especially clever one.

Jack saw a boy leave the group and advance toward him. He felt a little apprehension when he recognized Bailey, the smart shortstop of the famous Harmony nine. What did this mean? Could it be possible that those fellows of the other town had gotten "cold feet" after the last game, and were about to withdraw from the match to play out the tie?

Jack could hardly believe such a thing possible. He knew and respected Martin, the gentlemanly captain of the rival team, too well, to think he would show the white feather. Why, it would be talked about all through the county, and Harmony could never again make any boast. Oh! no, something of a minor nature must have come up, and Martin wished to consult with the captain of the Chester nine in advance–possibly some local ground rule had been framed which, in all honor, he believed the others ought to know about before the time came to apply it.

"Hello! Jack!" said Bailey with the easy familiarity that boys in general show when dealing with one another, though they may even be comparative strangers.

"Glad to see you, Bailey," returned the other. "What brings you over this way again? Anything new come up?"

None of the other players had followed Bailey when he advanced. They seemed to take it for granted that if it was any of their business, Jack would be sure to call them up.

"Why, something has happened that we thought you fellows ought to know about," continued the shortstop of the Harmony team, with a little trace of confusion in his manner.

"And Captain Martin sent you over as a messenger, is that it, Bailey?" asked Jack, shaking hands cordially; for he had liked the other chap through all the two games already played; Bailey was clean in everything he did, and that sort of a boy always appealed to Jack Winters, detesting fraud and trickery as he did.

"That's it, Jack. He gave me this note to deliver; and I'm to answer any questions you may see fit to ask."

There was something a bit queer in the other's manner as he said this; and the way in which he thrust out a sealed envelope at the same time smacked of the dramatic. Jack took it with rising curiosity. Really, this began to assume a more serious aspect than he had at first thought could be possible. It was therefore with considerable interest he tore off the end of the envelope, and pulled out the enclosure, which proved to be a full page of writing easily deciphered.

Since it is necessary that the contents of that missive should be understood by the reader we shall take the liberty of looking over Jack's shoulder and devouring Martin's letter as eagerly as the recipient did.

"To the Captain and Members of the Chester Baseball Team:

"We, the entire Harmony baseball organization, take this method of warning you that it is more than half suspected there is a miserable plot afloat to cause you fellows to lose the game next Saturday through a fluke. It may not be true, but we believe it to be our duty to put you on your guard, because we would disdain to profit by any such trickery bordering on a crime. There are some reckless sports up from the city, who have been wagering heavily on our winning out. After the game last Saturday, it seems that they have begun to get cold feet, and believe that Harmony might not have such a soft snap as they thought when they made all those heavy wagers. Needless to state the boys of the team do not share in their fears, for we are perfectly confident that we can down you again, as we did in the first game. But we would be ashamed if anything happened to cast the slightest doubt on the glory of our anticipated victory. We believe you Chester fellows to be an honorable lot and no matter whoever wins we want it to be a victory as clean and honest as they make them. We intend to have men on the watch for crooked business. One thing we beg you to do, which is to set a guard on your water-bucket, and *allow no one not a player on your side to go anywhere near it!* There have been occasions on record where dope was given through the drinking water, that made players sick, and unable to do their best in the game, thus losing for their side.

"We send you this, believing that you will give us full credit for being lovers of clean sport. So keep in the pink of condition for Saturday, and able to do your prettiest, for, believe us, you will have need of every ounce of ability you possess, because Hendrix says he never felt more fit in his life.

> Signed   CAPTAIN LEM MARTIN,
> For the entire Harmony Baseball Team."

When Jack had finished reading this remarkable letter, the first thing he did was characteristic of the boy–he reached out his hand toward Bailey.

"Shake again, Bailey! I honor such sentiments, and believe me, the boys of Chester will never forget such a friendly spirit as your team shows. We, too, would refuse to play in a game where we had the slightest reason to believe crooked work was going on, that would be to the disadvantage of our adversaries."

The little shortstop's eyes glistened as he wrung Jack's hand.

"Glad to see you take it in the right spirit, old fellow," he hastened to say. "We were horribly worked up when we got wind of this business through sheer accident. Only a mean skunk like a tricky sport from the city could dream of doing such a thing. But now it's come out, you'll find that all Harmony will be on edge looking for signs of treachery toward you fellows."

"How about telling the other boys?" inquired Jack.

"You're at perfect liberty to do that," the shortstop assured him. "In fact, we expected you would. The sooner the news is carried through Chester the better chance that nothing so low-down will be attempted; and no matter how the game turns out, it will be clean. Much as we want to win we all agree that we'd rather be badly licked by Chester than have it ever said there was a shadow of fraud on our victory."

So Jack beckoned to the rest.

"Only the members of the team, subs. as well as regulars, are wanted here!" he called aloud; and accordingly, they came forward, most of the boys exchanging looks of natural curiosity, and doubtless fearing that some hitch had occurred in the programme for the ensuing Saturday.

Judge of their amazement when Jack read aloud the letter from Captain Martin. It seemed almost unbelievable to some of the boys. Others who always made it a practice to glean all the baseball news in the city papers that came to certain Chester homes, may have known that such evil practices had been attempted occasionally, especially where unprincipled men began to wager money on the result of championship games.

All of them seemed unanimously of the opinion that Harmony had evinced a most laudable and sportsmanlike spirit in sending this strange warning. It made them feel that in struggling for the mastery on the diamond with such manly fellows, they were up against the right kind of foe-men. Indeed, even a defeat at the hands of Harmony would not seem so dreadful a disaster, now that they knew Martin and his crowd to be such good fellows.

Bailey did not wait to listen to many of the remarks that followed the reading of the letter. He could see that Chester had received the warning in the same friendly spirit in which it had been sent; and this was the news he meant to carry back with him.

 "I want to own up they're a pretty decent bunch of ball players after all!" declared Phil Parker, who had been known to say a few hard things about the hustling Harmony boys after that first game, in which Jack's team was given such a lively set-back.

"Glad you've found that out, Phil," remarked Steve Mullane, drily. "Next time don't be so quick to judge your opponents. Because a chap happens to be a hustler on the baseball or football field, isn't a sign that he's anything of a brute in private life. Only the hustlers succeed on the diamond. Umpire-baiters are sometimes the kind of men who are bullied by a little bit of a woman at home."

"That's right for you, Steve!" declared Herbert Jones, nodding his head in the affirmative. "I've got an uncle who used to be known as a regular scorcher on the gridiron, and who gained the name of a terror; but, say, you ought to see that big hulk wash dishes for Mrs. Jones, who can walk under his arm. Why, in private life he's as soft as mush, and his fog-horn voice is toned down to almost the squeak of a fiddle when he sings the baby to sleep. It isn't always safe to judge a man by what he does when he's playing ball."

"But just think of the meanness of those men wanting to put some kind of dope in our drinking water!" ejaculated Fred Badger in evident anger. "Why, they might have made some of us real sick in the bargain, as well as lost us the game. Such scoundrels ought to be locked up; they're a menace to any community."

"Well, Harmony town is responsible for pretty much all of this," suggested Jack. "They are letting things go along over there that sleepy old Chester never would think of permitting. Those who sow the wind must expect to reap the whirlwind sooner or later."

"Yes," added Toby Hopkins, with a snort, "they seemed to think it gave tone to their games to have those city men come up and back Harmony with money. Let's hope that after the lesson our worthy mayor set them last Saturday and with this disgrace threatening their good name those Harmony folks will get busy cleaning their Augean stables before any real harm is done."

Every one had an opinion, and yet they were pretty much along similar lines. The Chester boys thought it terrible that such a warning had to be sent out; though of course they all gave Martin and his crowd full credit for doing the right thing.

Jack was interested in watching Fred Badger, and listening to what he had to say from time to time. Apparently Fred was as indignant as any of them, and so far as Jack could tell there was not a particle of sham about his fervent denunciation of the evil deed contemplated by those strangers anxious to beat the Chester people, who wagered with them, out of their money.

And yet what else could be expected of such men, accustomed to evil ways, and earning their money at race-tracks and the like? What of a boy who had the confidence of his mates on the team, conspiring to sell them out for a bribe? Jack fairly writhed as he thought of it. Looking at Fred's earnest face as he spoke he could not bring himself to fully believe the other capable of attempting such a dastardly trick; and yet Jack had his fears all the same.

CHAPTER XI
SITTING ON THE LID

The troubles and tribulations of the captain of a baseball team are many, and ofttimes peculiar, as Jack was fast finding out. A load of responsibility rests on his shoulders such as none of the other players knows. He must watch every fellow, and notice the slightest deterioration in his playing; be ready to chide, or give encouraging words; and lie awake nights cudgeling his brains to discover a way of getting better work out of certain delinquent members of the nine, or else making way for a substitute who gives promise of being worth his salt.

Jack was already having troubles enough, he thought, what with the petty annoyances, his grave suspicions of Fred Badger's loyalty, and now this prospect of foul play being attempted by those evil-disposed men from the city, only bent on reaping a harvest of money from the outcome of the game. There was more to come for the boy who was "sitting on the lid," it turned out.

Donohue had been acting somewhat queerly during the last two days, Jack noticed. True enough, he came to the practice games, and seemed to have all of his old cunning in his arm when they had him pitch, striking out men at pleasure; but he never smiled, would draw off to himself frequently, and was seen to shake his head as though his thoughts could not be any too pleasant.

What could be ailing the boy, Jack wondered? Surely after his wonderful and even brilliant work in the box on the preceding Saturday, Alec was not beginning to doubt his ability to turn back those sluggers on Harmony's roll. No, Jack concluded that it could not be this.

"I've just *got* to get Alec by himself, and have it out with him!" he told Toby, with whom he had been earnestly discussing the matter. "Whatever is troubling the boy, the sooner it's laid the better; for if he keeps on in the frame of mind he seems to be in just now, it's bound to affect his work when we want him to be at his very best."

"That's the only way to do, Jack," his chum assured him. "Get Alec by himself, and talk to him like a Dutch uncle. Nobody can do it as well as you, I'm sure. And, Jack, if there's any way I can help, any of us, in fact, remember you've only got to speak. Every fellow on the nine would work his fingers to the bone to please you. And, besides, we've got our hearts set on winning that game. It would mean the making of Chester as a town where clean sport for boys is indulged in."

Jack therefore watched until he saw Alec Donohue put on his coat and saunter off, as though heading for home. Then he proceeded to follow after the pitcher.

"I'm going your way, Alec," he remarked, when the other turned his head and lifted his eyebrows in some little surprise at discovering the captain of the nine trotting along in his wake. "Besides, I want to have a nice little talk with you while we have the chance."

Young Donohue flushed a bit.

"I rather half expected you'd say that, Jack," he remarked, with a tinge of distress in his voice. "But, after all, the sooner it's over with the better, I reckon. I was trying to muster up enough courage to speak to you about it this afternoon, but I felt too hanged bad even to get started."

Jack became alarmed.

"I've noticed that you seemed anything but happy lately, Alec," he hastened to say, as he threw an arm across the shoulders of the pitcher, "and it began to bother me a heap; because I know a pitcher can hardly deliver his best goods unless he's feeling as fit as a fiddle. What's gone wrong? I hope you're not feeling sick, or anything like that?"

Alec swallowed hard before starting to make answer to this question.

"Never felt better in my whole life, Jack, so far as my body goes; and, if I do say it myself, I firmly believe I'd be able to do better work on Saturday than any of you have ever seen me give. But I'm in a peck of trouble at home, and I'm terribly afraid that I won't be able to pitch again for Chester."

"How is that, Alec!" asked the other, solicitously.

"Why, I may not be living in the town on Saturday, you see, and one of the rules of our match games is that every player shall be a resident of the town his club represents. My folks are going to move to Harmony on Friday, sure!"

"That's bad for us, Alec," admitted Jack, his heart sinking as he remembered how ineffectual McGuffey had been in the box even while Chester was scoring against the Harmony man; and with Hendrix sending his puzzling shoots over, defeat was positive for

Chester unless they had Donohue to depend on. "Tell me how it happens, will you?"

"Why, my father lost his job a few weeks back, being sick for a spell. He doesn't seem able to strike anything here, but is promised a good job up in Harmony on condition that he moves there right away, so he can start in Saturday. And, Jack, he said this morning that much as he hated to leave town, there wasn't any other way out; so we're going the day after tomorrow. I knew I'd have to tell you, but, say, every time I tried to speak it seemed like I'd choke."

It was a time for quick thinking with Jack.

"I wish you could hold this off for just twenty-four hours, Alec," he told the other. "Perhaps I may find a way out long before then. Could you promise me that?"

"Sure thing, Jack, and believe me I'd be mighty happy if only you did run across a way of bridging this trouble. But we're out of money at home, and jobs don't seem to be floating around in Chester, at least for men as old as my dad."

"Would you mind telling me what he was promised over at Harmony?" continued the other, at which question Alec started, and looked eagerly at him.

"Why, you see, all my dad's fit for these days, with his rheumatism bothering him, is a job as night watchman in some factory or mill. That was what he has been promised in Harmony."

"And what wages does he expect to draw down, Alec? I'm not asking from any curiosity, remember, but I ought to know if I'm going to try to get your father a position here in his old town where he's known so well and respected; and where his eldest son is making such a name for himself as a sterling baseball player."

"He is promised twenty-one a week, Jack. You see, in these times wages have all gone up to meet the high cost of living. Time was when he only got fifteen per. I reckon now, it's your plan to interview some of the gentlemen who are interested in baseball, and that you hope they'll consent to give my dad a steady job so as to keep the Donohue family in Chester. Well, here's hoping you strike luck, Jack. If you do I'll be the happiest boy in Chester tonight, and ready to pitch my arm off Saturday so as to bring another Harmony scalp home."

They shook hands heartily, and then Jack scurried away. It was one of his cardinal principles never to delay when he had anything of importance on his hands. So a short time later he entered one of the big hives of industry that was managed by Mr. Charles Taft, a middle-aged gentleman who seemed greatly interested in the rise of boys' sports in Chester, and who had already favored Jack on several occasions.

It was partly through his generosity that the team had been able to secure suits and outfits in the way of bats, balls, bases, and such things, when the season began. More than that, it was this same Mr. Taft who had gladly agreed to let one of his workers have an occasional afternoon off duty when his services were required to coach the struggling ball players, sadly in need of professional advice and encouragement.

When the boy was ushered into his private office, the stout gentleman held out his hand, and smiled pleasantly. He was a great and constant admirer of Jack Winters, because he could read frankness, honesty, determination to succeed, and many other admirable traits in the boy's face. In fact, Mr. Taft had been quite an athlete himself when at college, and his interest in clean sport had never flagged even when he took up serious tasks in the business world.

"Glad to see you, my boy," he observed, in his customary genial fashion, as he squeezed Jack's hand. "What can I do for you today? How is the team getting along after that glorious game you played? No press of business is going to prevent one man I know of in Chester from attending the game next Saturday. I hope you are not in any trouble, Jack?"

Evidently his quick eye had noted the slight cloud on the boy's face, an unusual circumstance in connection with the captain of the nine.

"Yes, I am in a peck of trouble, sir," candidly confessed Jack. "The fact of the matter is it looks as though, we might be short our wonderful young pitcher, Alec Donohue, next Saturday."

"How's that, Jack?" demanded the gentleman, anxiously. "I'm greatly interested in that lad's work. He certainly has the making of a great pitcher in him. Why, if we lose Donohue, I'm afraid the cake will be dough with us, for I hear Hendrix is in excellent shape, and declares he will pitch the game of his life when next he faces your crowd."

"I'll tell you what the matter is, sir," and with that Jack plunged into a brief exposition of the Donohue family troubles.

As he proceeded, he saw with kindling joy that a beaming smile had commenced to creep over the rosy countenance of the one-time college athlete. This encouraged him to state how a wild hope had arisen in his heart that possibly some job might be found for Mr. Donohue that would keep the family in Chester right along.

"We need him the worst kind, Mr. Taft," he concluded. "If Alec quits us cold I'm afraid it's bound to set all our fine schemes for athletics in Chester back a peg or two. This seems to be a most critical time with us. If we win that game we're going to make many new friends around here, who will assist us in getting that club-house we've been talking about, and putting athletic sports on a sound footing in our town."

"Make your mind easy, Jack, my boy," said the stout gentleman, with a nod, "Alec will toss for us next Saturday, because we won't allow the Donohue family to shake the dust of Chester off their shoes. Why, it happens that my night watchman has just given notice that he must throw up his job because he has taken a position in one of those munition works in another town, where they pay such big wages for men who know certain things. So consider that I offer Donohue the position at twenty-four dollars a week; and there's no reason why it shouldn't be a permanent job, as I understand he's a reliable watchman."

Jack could hardly speak for happiness. The tears actually came in his eyes as he wrung the hand of the gentleman.

"Oh! you don't know how happy you've made me by saying that, Mr. Taft," he managed to declare. "And have I permission to go over to the Donohue home with that glorious news right away?"

"Suit yourself about that, son. Tell him to come around tomorrow and see me; but that the job is his right now. And also tell Alec from me that Chester expects him to fool those heavy hitters of Harmony to the top of his bent, when he faces Hutchings, Clifford, Oldsmith, O'Leary and the rest."

When Jack went out of that office his heart was singing with joy. The clouds had rolled away once more, and the future looked particularly bright. He only hoped it would be an augury of success in store for the Chester nine in their coming battle.

CHAPTER XII
ONE TROUBLE AFTER ANOTHER

"Ting-a-ling!"

The telephone bell in Jack's home was ringing just as the boy passed through the hall on Thursday morning around ten. He had been busily engaged in matters at home, and not gone out up to then. As he held his ear to the receiver he caught the well-known voice of Toby Hopkins.

"That you, Jack?"

"No one else; and what's going on over at your house?" Jack replied. "I thought for sure you'd have been across before now, if only to learn how I came out with that Donohue trouble."

"Oh! I would have been starting you up at daybreak this morning, Jack, only it happens that I learned the good news last night."

"How was that?" demanded the other; "did you walk over to their place to ask Alec about it?"

"I went over to offer Mr. Donohue a job in the Cameron mill tending a plane, only to have him tell me with a happy look in his eyes that he had already taken a position as night watchman with the foundry and rolling mill people, meaning Mr. Taft, your special friend and backer. So I knew you had been busy as well as myself. But you can tell me all about it, and what the Donohues said, when you join me inside of five minutes; because I'm coming over in our tin-Lizzie to take you on a little jaunt with me."

"But I don't believe I ought to go off just now," expostulated Jack; "because I've got a number of things to see to; and besides, we must be out to practice again this afternoon."

"Rats! you've got plenty of time for all that," snorted Toby, who evidently would not take no for an answer when once his heart was set on a thing. "And, besides, it happens that I'm heading for Harmony this time, on some business for dad. We can come back by the road that finally skirts the lake shore. I heard some of the fellows say they meant to go swimming this morning, and we'll like as not come across them in the act, perhaps have a dip ourselves for diversion. Say you'll go, Jack?"

It was a very alluring programme for a boy who loved the open as much as Jack did. His scruples vanished like the mist before the morning sun.

"All right, then, Toby," he went on to say; "I'll go with you, because we can kill two birds with one stone. It happens that I'd like to have a chat with Martin, the Harmony captain. There are several things we ought to settle before we meet on the diamond Saturday afternoon. I'll be ready for you when you come around with your antique chariot."

"It isn't good taste to look a gift-horse in the mouth, Jack; and you ought to know that same flivver can show her heels to many a more pretentious car when on the road. So-long, then. See you in five minutes!"

Toby was as good as his word, and the car stopped before Jack's gate with much honking of the claxon. Once they were off of course Toby demanded that his companion relate his experiences of the preceding afternoon, when he interviewed the affable manager of the big rolling mills, and secured that offer of a good job for Mr. Donohue, calculated to keep their wonderful wizard of a pitcher on the roll-call of the Chester baseball team.

"Of course," said Jack, in conclusion, "when I got to Alec's place and told them what good news I was fetching, they were all mighty well pleased. I thought Alec would certainly have a fit, he danced around so. And take it from me, Toby, that boy will show the Harmony players some wonderful tricks from his box when they face him again, because he's feeling simply immense. When a pitcher is in the pink of condition, he can make the heaviest sluggers feed from his hand; and Alec certainly has a bunch of shoots that run all the way from speed, curves, drops, and several others that, for one, I never before heard of. Now tell me about your offer of a job."

Toby laughed softly.

"Well, you see, Jack, I just knew what you'd be up to, and says I to myself, it'd be a bully thing if I could beat Jack out for just once. So I humped myself and ran around to see Joe Cameron, who happens to be a distant relative of my mother, you remember. He wanted to help me, but at first couldn't see any way where he could make use of a man like Donohue, at least at living wages. But I pleaded so hard, that in the end he remembered a certain place that was vacant. True, it only paid fifteen a week, but he placed it at my disposal. And so after supper I ran around to see if Donohue wouldn't consent to fill that job, through the summer, or until a better one showed up. But I was tickled when Alec told me about your stunt."

Chatting as they rode along, they were not long in reaching Harmony. This town was somewhat larger than Chester, though the latter did more business when it came to the matter of dollars and cents, on account of the mills and factories along the lake and the river.

Toby soon transacted his errand, which was connected with a business house. Then they made inquiries, and learned that Martin lived on the outskirts of the town, actually on the road they meant to take going home by another route.

"That must be his place yonder!" remarked Toby, presently.

"No doubt about it," laughed Jack, "for you can see that a baseball crank lives in that big house with the extensive grounds. Listen to the plunk of a ball landing in a glove, will you. Martin is having a little private practice of a morning on his own account."

"Yes, I can see two fellows passing the ball across the lawn," admitted Toby. "If all the other members of the Harmony team are just as hard at work every hour of daylight, it's mighty evident they mean to be as fit as a fiddle for that big game. They must feel that if they lose, all their good work of the summer will go in the scrap heap."

"I'm glad to know they feel so anxious," chuckled Jack. "It shows how we made them respect our team that last time, when they had their full line-up on deck. We are due for a thrilling game, and don't you forget it, Toby."

When the two boys who were passing the ball so swiftly discovered the stopping flivver, and recognized their morning callers, they hurried out through the gate to shake hands with Jack and Toby. Martin's companion proved to be Hutchings, the efficient first baseman and hard hitter of the locals.

They chatted for some time, Jack making such, inquiries as he had in mind, and being given all the information at the disposal of the other pair.

"About that letter of mine," Captain Martin finally remarked, when the visitors were preparing to depart; "it was a nasty subject to handle, and I hardly knew how to go about it; so finally decided to hit straight out, and tell you what we suspected was going on over here. I was glad to hear from Bailey that you boys took it in just the same spirit it was sent."

"We were in a humor to give you and your fellows a hearty cheer," Jack told him; "we all agreed that it was a genuine pleasure to run up against such a fine bunch of honorable ball players; and believe me, if we can't carry off that game for Chester, we'll not begrudge your crowd for taking it, because we know it will have been fairly won."

It was in this friendly spirit that the rival captains shook hands and parted. Each leader would fight tooth and nail to capture the impending game, using all legitimate means to further his ends; but there would be no hard feelings between the opposing players. Harmony's fine act had rendered this a certainty.

Jack had said nothing about the narrow escape Chester had from a real catastrophe in the loss of their wonderful young pitcher. He thought it best not to mention matters that concerned only Chester folks; although feeling positive that Martin would congratulate him on his success in keeping Alec; for the game would lose much of its interest if only a second-string pitcher officiated in the box for either side when they anticipated showing their best goods.

"He's all wool, and a yard wide, that Martin," asserted Toby, after they had turned their faces toward home again, and were booming along the road that presently would take them close to the shore of Lake Constance.

"There's no doubt about his being a good fellow," agreed Jack; "and it's certainly a real pleasure to go up against such a crowd. For one, I've underestimated the Harmony boys. We've heard a lot about their noisy ways and hustle, but, after all, I think most of it's on the surface, and deeper down they're just as much gentlemen as you'd find anywhere. Most games of rivalry are won through aggressiveness, and plenty of fellows cultivate that mode of playing. It doesn't follow that such chaps are boors, or clowns, or brawlers off the field. We could stand a little more of that sort of thing ourselves, to tell you the truth, Toby—standing on our toes, and keeping wide awake every second of the time play is on."

"Right you are, Jack, and after this I'm going to whoop it up a lot more'n I've ever done before. You'll see some *hopping* to beat the band, too. I've managed to cover a good deal of territory up to now but, say, I aspire to do still better. I'm rubbing snake oil on my joints right along so as to make 'em more supple. Why, I'd *bathe* in it if I thought that would make me better able to do my part toward corraling that great game for Chester."

"There, I had a first glimpse of Lake Constance," remarked Jack. "The trees have closed the vista again, so you can't catch it; but I suppose we'll soon come to a place where we'll have the water on our left, and the road even runs along close to the edge. I remember skating up about this far last February, soon after I arrived in Chester; and the lake was then a solid sheet of smooth ice."

"Queer how cold the water stays all summer," mused Toby. "There are times when I've seen boys shivering in July and August while bathing. It's fed by springs, they say, though Paradise River also empties into the lake. There, now you can see away across to the other shore, Jack. Isn't it a bully sheet of water, though?"

"What dandy times we can have next winter iceboating, skating, playing hockey, and everything like that," suggested Jack, delightedly, as his eyes feasted on the immense body of fresh water, with its surface just rippled in the soft summer breeze.

"We'll soon come to where the boys said they meant to go in swimming this morning," added Toby. "It's a perfect day, too, even if the sun does feel hot. Just such a day as this when I got that nasty little cramp in the cold water of the lake, and might have had a serious time only for Big Bob Jeffries taking me on his back and carrying me like a baby to the shore."

"Listen!" exclaimed Jack just then, "what's all that yell going on ahead of us? The boys must be cutting up capers; and yet it strikes me there's a note of fear in their shouts. Turn on the juice, Toby, and eat up the road! Something terrible may be happening, you know. Things keep following each other these days like sheep going over a fence after their leader!"

Toby made the flivver fairly bound along, such was his eagerness to arrive at the scene of all the excitement. Twenty seconds later he gave a loud cry.

"Look, Jack, there's some one floundering out there, and throwing up his arms. It's our Joel Jackman, I do believe! and great Cæsar! he's got a cramp and is drowning!"

CHAPTER XIII
WHEN THE CRAMP SEIZED JOEL

What the excited Toby had just said in thrilling tones was undoubtedly the truth. There was no "fooling" about the frantic actions of the boy who was struggling so desperately out in the lake. He was threshing the water furiously, now vanishing partly underneath, only to come up again in a whirl of bubbles.

When a cramp seizes any one, no matter if he should happen to be a champion in the art of swimming, he is always in mortal peril of his life, especially should he be at some distance from the shore, and in deep water. It almost paralyzes every muscle, and the strongest becomes like a very babe in its spasmodic clutch.

Joel Jackman was long-legged and thin, but had always been reckoned one of those wiry sort of chaps, built on the order of a greyhound. He could run like the wind, and jump higher than any fellow in all Chester, barring none. But when that awful cramp seized him in the cold water of Lake Constance, lie found himself unable to make any progress toward shore, distant at least fifty feet.

It was all he could do to keep his head above water, struggling as he was with the fear of a terrible death before his eyes. His two comrades were running up and down on the shore; not that they were such arrant cowards but what they would have been willing to do almost anything to help Joel; but unfortunately they had lost their heads in the sudden shock; and as Toby afterwards contemptuously said, "acted like so many chickens after the ax had done its foul work."

Jack sized up the situation like a flash.

"Toby, you get one of those boards over yonder, and come out to help me if I'm in trouble, understand?" he jerked out, even as the flivver came to a sudden stop, and he was bounding over the side regardless of any exit.

"All right, Jack; you bet I will!" Toby shouted, following suit.

Jack began to shed his outer clothes as he ran swiftly forward. First his cap went, and then his coat. He had low shoes on so that he was able to detach them with a couple of quick jerks, and at the loss of the laces.

Two seconds, when at the verge of the water, sufficed for him to get rid of his trousers, and then, he went in with a rush.

Toby meanwhile had tried to follow suit even as he made for the boards in question. It had been just like Jack to glimpse these in the beginning, while those other fellows apparently did not know a board was within half a mile.

Seeing what Toby meant to do, the two swimmers followed suit, so that presently the whole three of them had each picked up a plank, and were pushing out with it.

Jack had plunged ahead, swimming in any old way, since his one object just then was speed, and not style. He could not have done better had he been up against a swarm of rivals working for a prize. Well, there *was* a prize dangling there in plain sight. A precious human life was at stake, and unless he could arrive in time poor Joel might go down, never to come up again in his senses.

He had already been under once, and through his desperate efforts succeeded in reaching the surface of the agitated water again. Even as Jack started swimming, after getting in up to his neck, the drowning boy vanished again.

Jack swam on, trying to increase his pace, if such a thing were possible. He must get on the spot without the waste of a second. Joel would likely come to the surface again, but battling more feebly against the threatening fate. If he went down a third time it would be all over but the funeral, Jack knew.

He was more than two-thirds of the way there when to his ecstatic joy he once more discovered the head of Joel. The boy was still making a gallant fight, but under a fearful handicap.

Jack shouted hoarsely as he swam onward:

"Keep fighting, Joel! We'll get you, old chap! Strike out as hard as you can! You're all right, I tell you, only don't stop working!"

Perhaps these cheering words did help Joel to continue his weakening efforts to keep himself afloat. Possibly had it not been for his hearing Jack's voice raised in encouragement, he might have given up the ghost before then.

Nearer Jack surged, his heart seeming to be in his throat with dread lest Joel go down again a few seconds before he could get within touch. The three boys with the boards were also coming along in a solid bunch, although of course with less speed than Jack showed, owing partly to the fact that they had to shove the planks before them.

Now, Joel, with a last despairing gurgle was sinking again, and for the very last time, being utterly exhausted by his frantic struggles, and the terrible pain occasioned by the cramp.

But Jack knew he had arrived close enough to dart forward and clutch his comrade before the other could quite vanish from view. Joel was so far gone that he did not try to grip his rescuer, as most drowning persons will do in their frantic desire to save themselves at any cost.

Jack tried to keep the boy's head above water as best he could. He made no effort to swim towards the shore. What was the use when the other fellows were coming along with their boards. The one thing necessary just then was to prevent Joel from swallowing any more water; he had already no doubt gulped in huge quantities, and lost the ability to breathe properly.

So Toby and the other two found them when they finally arrived. The planks were arranged so that Joel could be raised and sustained by their means; after which the little procession of swimmers headed for the bank.

When they arrived, Joel was lifted out of the water and carried tenderly up to a patch of green sward lying in the shade of a wide-branching oak. Here they laid him down on his chest, while Jack proceeded to work over him, instructing the other fellows just what they were to do to assist.

He knelt astride with one knee on either side of Joel's body, and commenced pressing down regularly on the small of his back, so as to induce an artificial respiration. At the same time, Toby and one of the other fellows worked the unconscious boy's arms back and forth like a pair of pistons; while the third fellow started to rub his cold lower extremities.

At first Joel seemed pretty far gone, and his appearance sent a chill through the sympathetic heart of Toby Hopkins. But after they had kept up this vigorous treatment for a little while, there were signs of returning animation. Joel belched out a gallon of water, Toby always insisted, and inside of ten minutes was able to talk, though Jack insisted on keeping up the rubbing until the boy's body was a rosy hue from the irritation.

"Now get some clothes on, Joel, and you'll soon be feeling prime," he told the other, whose lips were still blue and quivering.

Joel had had quite enough of swimming for one day. Indeed, he would be pretty cautious about getting any distance away from the shore after that, having received a most fearful shock. Still, boys recover from such things, given a little time, and Joel had always been reckoned a fellow who did not know the meaning of the word "fear."

The other boys had apparently lost the joy of bathing for that day. They, too, started to don their clothes, and begged Toby to "hold up," so that they might get a lift to town in the flivver; which, being a whole-souled fellow, of course, "Hop" was only too glad to do.

Later on, after arriving home, Jack and Toby talked matters over between themselves. This new and entirely unexpected happening had been only another link in the growing chain of troubles hanging over the head of the captain of the Chester baseball team.

"What if we hadn't chanced to be on the road just at that very minute, Jack?" ventured Toby, with a shiver; "poor old Joel would certainly have been drowned, because neither Frank nor Rufus had the slightest idea what to do so as to save him. And that would have broken up our combination in the nine, all right, because we'd find it hard to replace such a runner and fielder and batter as Joel."

"Of course," said Jack, "the worst thing of all would be losing a friend. Joel is a mighty fine all-around fellow, and most of us are fond of him. And just as you say, the game would like as not have to be postponed, because how could we play as we would want to with a chum lying dead at home? So I'm grateful because we did chance to be Johnny-on-the-spot."

"That was sure a great job you did, Jack, believe me; and when I say such a thing I'm not meaning to throw bouquets either. Whee! but you did shoot through the water like a fish. I've watched a pickerel dart at a minnow, but no slinker ever had the bulge on you that time."

"I had to get along with all sail set," Jack told him, with a smile, for it is always pleasant to have a friend hand out a meed of praise, even to the most modest boy going. "I knew Joel was at the last gasp, and even a second lost might mean he'd go down for the third time before I could get there. And yet do you know, Toby, it seemed to me right then and there as if I had a ton of lead fastened to me. Why, I felt as though something was holding me back, just as you know the nightmare grips you usually. But when I was within striking distance, I knew I could save Joel. He made a gallant fight, and deserves a lot of praise."

"I wonder what we'll have happen next, Jack? Seems to me not a day passes but you've got to play the rescue act with some member of our team. There was Fred worrying you, and still acting queer; then along comes Donohue threatening to give us the slip because his folks meant to move out of town, and he couldn't pitch unless he lived in Chester. Now, as if those things didn't count up enough to keep you awake nights, old Joel had to go and try to kick the bucket, and force you to yank him out of the lake."

Jack laughed and shook his head.

"It's hard to tell what another day may bring forth, Toby," he went on to say. "Remember, this is only Thursday, and Friday is said to be a very unlucky day in some people's lives, especially when it falls on the thirteenth of the month, as happens this year. There are still a few fellows in the nine who haven't shown up yet in the catastrophe ward. Why, Toby, it might even be *you* who'll wave the flag and call out for help."

"I give you my affidavit, Jack, that I'm going to play mighty safe from now on. No fishing or swimming for me, and I'll even run that old flivver at slow speed, for fear it takes a notion to land me in a ditch, and come in on top of me. But I hope, Jack, you're not getting discouraged with all these things coming right along?"

"I might, Toby, if I were not built on a stubborn line. We'll go to Harmony on Saturday and make a fight for that game even if we have to lug along a crippled nine, some of them on crutches!"

Toby brightened up on hearing the leader grimly say this.

"That's the sort of stuff, Jack!" he exclaimed, slapping his chum on the back.

"In the bright lexicon of youth there is no such word as fail! We'll go forth with our hearts set on victory, and that's one half of the battle. Hurrah! for Chester!"

CHAPTER XIV
A NIGHT ALARM

Before the two boys parted that afternoon, after the practice of the whole regular nine, barring Joel, who, taking Jack's advice, laid off for one occasion, Joel had asked the captain to drop over when he had finished his supper.

"I want to see you about a number of things," he had told Jack; "not so much in connection with the game we're scheduled to play, as other affairs looking to the ambitious programme we've mapped out for Chester boys the rest of the summer, in the fall, and even up to winter. For one thing, I'd like to give you a few pointers about the fellows in our crowd, so that you can size them up for the football squad later on."

That caught Jack in a weak spot.

"I'll go you there, Toby," he hastened to say, "because I've been trying to figure things out along those lines myself. When you're placing men on an eleven, you ought to know their every strong and weak point; and I'm too new a hand here in Chester to be on to such things. So I'll be glad to have you give me points."

Accordingly, he knocked at the Hopkins' door soon after seven that evening, and was immediately admitted by Toby himself. The Hopkins family consisted of Toby's father and mother, and an older son just then away on a trip to the West, as he was attending college, and had been promised this treat if he passed with honors. There was also a very small girl, named Tessie, who naturally was the pet of the household, and in a way to be spoiled by the adoration of her two brothers.

Toby had a den of his own in the upper part of the rambling house. Here just as most boys love to do, he had the walls fairly covered with the burgees of various colleges, all sorts of mementos collected during his outdoor experiences, curios that in Toby's eyes were precious because many of them bore an intimate relation with some little adventure or jolly outing in which he had taken part.

There were also football togs, baseball contraptions, fishing paraphernalia in unlimited abundance, as well as striking illustrations covering the field of sport as seen through the eyes of youth.

But one good thing about it all, you would look in vain for the slightest trace of any vulgar picture; Toby had no love for such so-called sport as prize fighting or any kindred subject.

Here in this adorable den, reflecting the loves of a genuine boy with red blood in his veins, there often assembled a number of lads who always felt very much at home amidst such surroundings; but Toby would allow of no rough-house scuffling in his quarters, to annoy his mother, and get on her nerves. When the fellows dropped in to have a chat and lounge in his easy chairs amidst such exhilarating surroundings they were expected to behave themselves.

Joel had the big lamp lighted. It threw a fine mellow glow over the walls of the den and showed up the myriad of objects with which they were covered. Somehow, Joel always liked his room much better when that royal lamp was burning, for even the most remote corner, seldom pierced by the intercepted rays of the sun, loomed up under its ardent rays.

Here the pair settled down for a long quiet chat. Jack wanted to ask a hundred questions bearing on the boys with whom he had become so intimately associated during the few months since his advent in Chester. Since they had so kindly bestowed the leadership in sports upon him, he wished to be like a wise general and lose no opportunity for learning each boy's individual ability.

Of course he had been keeping close "tabs" on them right along, but then, Toby, who had seen them attempting to play football, for instance, would be able to tell of certain stunts this or that fellow had done that were out of the common. Such points help amazingly in "putting a round man in a round hole." Too often a half-back should be a tackle, or a guard, in order to bring out the very best that is in him.

Then again Toby knew more or less concerning the fighting abilities of the teams in the neighboring towns, Marshall and Harmony in particular. His love for sport had taken Toby to every game within thirty miles he could hear of in contemplation; for if Chester seemed bound to sleep, and decline to enter the lists, a fellow who yearned to indulge in such things must go abroad to satisfy his longings.

So it came about that he was able to give Jack many valuable tips connected with the elevens with whom Chester was apt to come in contact, should they succeed in whipping a team into anything like fair condition.

"Now, after all you've told me about our boys," Jack was saying along after nine o'clock, when he was thinking of starting home, feeling tired after such a strenuous day, "I begin to believe we can get up a squad of football players here capable of putting up a strong game. One thing in our favor is the fact that we have an old athlete like Coach Joe Hooker to show us how to work out greenhorns."

"That's as true as you live," snapped Toby, his face glowing with eagerness, for one of the ambitions of his life seemed in prospect of being fulfilled. "I've never really played football, though of course I can kick, and run, and dodge pretty fairly. But in theory I'm away up in the game. Other fellows are in the same fix; and we'll need a whole lot of practice before we feel justified in going up against any older eleven. Like as not we'll get snowed under; but even if we lose every game this season, it'll give us what we need in the way of experience, and another year we'll show the way."

"There are lots of other outdoor games we'll have to take up in season," continued Jack, thoughtfully. "Once the spirit of sport has gripped the boys of Chester, and they'll be hungry to go into anything that means a test of endurance, skill or pluck."

"I suppose now you've played football before, Jack?" asked the other.

"Well, we had a pretty fair eleven in the city I came from, and I was lucky enough to belong to them," he said modestly. "I don't know that I shone as a star very much, but on the whole, we managed to keep up our end, and last year we pulled off the championship in our section of country."

"What position did you fill?" queried Toby.

"Our captain made a half-back of me," came the answer. "Somehow he seemed to believe I was better suited for that position than a tackle, though I wanted to be in the other place at the start. But it happened there were two sprinters better fitted than I was to hold down the job. So unless I run across a man who seems to show signs of being my superior in the field I've occupied, I suppose I'll continue to play half-back to the end of the chapter."

"Well," remarked Toby, as Jack made out to pick up his cap with the intention of leaving, since the hour was getting late, "one more day, and then what? A whole twenty-four hours for things to happen calculated to bust up our plans, and knock 'em galley-west. I wish, this was Friday night, and nothing serious had come about. We need that big game to make us solid with the people of Chester. It might be hard on poor Harmony, but it would be the making of our town."

"Hearing you say that," chuckled Jack, "makes me think of that story of the old man and his boy's bull-pup."

"I don't know that I've ever heard it, so fire away and tell the yarn, Jack," the other pleaded.

"Why, once a boy had a young bull-pup of which he was very fond. His father also took considerable interest in teaching the dog new tricks. On one occasion the old man was down on his knees trying to make the small dog jump at him, while the boy kept sicking him on. Suddenly the bull-pup made a lunge forward and before the old man could draw back he had gripped him by the nose, and held on like fun. Then the boy, only thinking of how they had succeeded in tempting the small dog, clapped his hands and commenced to dance around, shouting: 'Swing him around, dad, swing him every which way! It's hard on you, of course, but I tell you it'll be the making of the pup!'"

Toby laughed as Jack finished the anecdote, which it happened he had never heard before.

"Well, Harmony will be dad, and the bull-pup I know turns out to be Chester, bent on holding through thick and thin to victory. I'm glad you came over, Jack, and if I've been able to hand you out a few pointers we haven't wasted our time."

"I noticed when on the way here that it had clouded up," remarked Jack. "Let's hope we don't get a storm that will compel us to postpone that game. Our boys are in the pink of condition, with so much practice, and might go stale by another week."

"That's another cause for anxiety, then," croaked Toby shrugging his shoulders. "Here, I'll find my cap, and step outdoors with you. My eyes are blinking after so much light, and a breath of fresh air wouldn't go bad."

He had hardly said this than Toby stopped in his tracks.

"Listen, Jack, the fire-alarm bell! There's a blaze starting up, and with so much wind blowing it may mean a big conflagration. Where did I toss that cap of mine?"

"I saw something like a cap behind the rowing-machine over there when I tried it out," observed the other, whose habit of noticing even the smallest things often served him well.

"Just what it is," asserted Toby, after making a wild plunge in the quarter designated; "that's my meanest trait, Jack. Mother tries to break me of it ever so often, but I seem to go back again to the old trick of carelessness. Now come on, and we'll rush out. Already I can hear people beginning to shout."

They went downstairs two at a jump. For once Toby did not think of his mother's nerves. Fires were not so frequent an occurrence in the history of a small city like Chester that a prospective conflagration could be treated lightly.

Once out of the house and they had no difficulty about deciding in which direction the fire lay. Some people, principally boys, were already running full-tilt through the street, and all seemed to be heading in the one direction. At the same time all manner of comments could be heard passing between them as they galloped along, fairly panting.

"It must be the big mill, from the light that's beginning to show up in the sky!" hazarded one boy.

"Shucks! what are you giving us, Sandy!" gasped another. "The mill ain't over in that direction at all. Only cottages lie there, with an occasional haystack belongin' to some garden-truck raiser. Mebbe it might be a barn."

"Just what it is, Tim," a third boy chimed in eagerly. "Hay burns like wildfire you know, and see how red the sky is agettin' now."

Neither Jack nor Toby had thus far ventured to make any sort of guess. No matter what was afire it promised to be a serious affair, with the wind blowing at the rate of twenty miles an hour or more. If it turned out to be a private house some one was likely to be rendered homeless before long.

The bell continued to clang harshly. Chester still clung to the volunteer system of firemen, though there was some talk of purchasing an up-to-date motor truck engine, and hiring a force to be on duty day and night.

"Jack," suddenly called out Toby, "don't you see that we're heading straight for Fred's house. Honest to goodness I believe it's that very cottage afire right now."

CHAPTER XV
WHAT HAPPENED AT THE FIRE

"Hello there, fellows, you're on the job, too, I see!"

That was burly Steve Mullane calling out as he came tearing along in the wake of Jack and Toby. Steve was passionately fond of anything in the line of a fire. He had been known to chase for miles out into the country on learning that some farmer's haystacks and barn were ablaze; though he usually arrived far too late to see anything but the ruins.

"What do you think, Steve," gurgled Toby, "I was just saying I thought it might be Fred Baxter's place."

"Seems like it was around that section of territory anyhow," replied the other, as well as he was able to speak, while exerting himself to the utmost.

Jack made no immediate comment, but he himself was beginning to believe Toby's guess might not be far wrong. It gave him a fresh wrench about the region of his heart to believe this. It would mean another source of trouble for poor Fred, and might in the end eliminate him from the game on Saturday.

All Chester was aroused by this time. When that brazen bell kept clanging away in such a loud fashion people knew that something out of the usual run was taking place. They flocked forth, all hurrying in the same general direction, until the streets were fairly blocked with the crowds.

Now came the engine, driven by an expert member of the fire company, the pair of horses galloping wildly under the whip, and the spur of such general excitement. Loud cheers greeted the advent of the volunteer department. The men looked very brave and heroic with their red firehats, and rubber coats. They would undoubtedly do good work once they got on the ground; but that wind was playing havoc with things, and perhaps after all it might not be possible to save the imperiled building.

All doubts were removed, for on rounding a bend the three boys discovered that it was actually the modest Badger house that was afire. Flames could be seen pouring out of the windows, and a great smoke arose, telling that the whole interior must be heating up, and liable to break into a vast blaze at any minute.

"Whee! it looks bad for Fred's folks, now!" cried Toby, his first thought being of the suffering of those involved.

"It's going to make a dandy fire, all right!" Steve was heard to say to himself; and it was not because he was a heartless boy that this was his first thought, for Steve could be as tender as the next one; only he did dearly love a fire, and on that account was apt to forget how a blaze almost always meant loss for somebody, possibly deadly peril as well.

There was quite a mob of people already on the spot. Some who lived much closer than the three chums had been able to reach the scene of the fire in considerably less time.

Jack was trying to remember what things looked like in the near vicinity of the Badger home. He had been there only once or twice in all, but that habit of observation clung to him, and he was thus able to recollect how he had noticed that some sort of a woodshed stood close to the back of the house. If this held considerable fuel for the kitchen stove, and a fire managed to start in some way, it was just situated right to sweep through the house, being on the windward end.

"Where's Fred and his folks?" asked Toby just then, as they started boy-fashion to elbow their way through the crowd, determined to get in the front rank in order to see everything that transpired.

Jack was himself looking eagerly around, with the same object in view. He remembered the sad face of Fred's little mother, who he feared had seen much of trouble during the later years of her life. It looked as though there might be still more cause for anxiety hovering over her.

"She must be in that bunch of women folks over yonder," asserted Steve. "Yes, I just had a glimpse of that pretty little kid, Fred's sister, Barbara. One of the women is holding the child in her arms, and she's wrapped in bed clothes, which shows she must have been sleeping when the fire broke out."

"I wonder what's happening over where that group of men is standing," remarked Toby, solicitously. "There, a boy has fetched a dipper of water from the well bucket. Why, somebody must have been hurt, Jack."

"Let's make our way over and find out," suggested Steve, quickly.

Accordingly the three boys pushed through the various groups of chattering men, women and children. The firemen had by now managed to get to work, and the first stream of water was playing on the burning house; though every one could see that there was little chance of saving any part of the doomed structure, since the fire fiend had gained such a start.

"What's the matter here?" Jack asked a small boy who came reeling out from the packed crowd, as though unable to look any longer.

"Why, it's Fred Badger!" he told them in his shrill piping tones that could be heard even above the hoarse cries of the fire laddies and the murmur of voices from the surging mob, constantly growing larger as fresh additions arrived.

"What happened to him?" almost savagely asked Steve.

"He was trying to haul some of the furniture out, I heard tell," continued the Chester urchin, "and he got hurted some way. He's lying there like he was dead. I just couldn't stand it any more, that's what."

Filled with horror Jack pushed forward, with his two chums backing him up. What fresh calamity was threatening the Badger family, he asked himself. Poor Fred certainly had quite enough to battle against without being knocked out in this fashion.

When, however, they had managed to press in close enough to see, it was to discover the object of their solicitude sitting up. Fred looked like a "drowned rat," as Toby hastened to remark, almost joyously. Evidently they had emptied the pail of cold water over his head in the effort to revive him, and with more or less success.

Jack was considerably relieved. It was not so bad as he had feared, though Fred certainly looked weak, and next door to helpless.

"I hope he'll not be knocked out from playing that game with us Saturday," Steve took occasion to say.

"Oh! Fred's made of tough stuff," asserted Toby, the wish being father to the thought; "he'll recover all right. I only hope they've got their goods covered by insurance. It'd be pretty rocky if they didn't, let me tell you. Nearly everything is gone, I'm afraid. Fred did manage to drag a little out, but that fire is bound to eat up the balance, no matter what the firemen can do to throw water inside."

Jack suddenly discovered that the man whom he had seen talking with Fred was pushing his way through the group. He acted too as though he might be deeply interested in matters, for he shoved folks aside with an air that would not stand for a refusal to allow him free passage. Toby discovered him at about the identical moment.

"Look who's here, Jack!" he muttered, tugging at the other's coat sleeve. "Now, what under the sun's gone and fetched that duck out here to bother Fred again? We really ought not allow such a thing, Jack. The nerve of the slick sport to push his way in to where Fred lies there."

"Just hold your horses, will you, Toby?" Jack told him. "As yet we don't know anything about that man, who or what life is, and the nature of his business with Fred. There, you see the boy seems to be glad to have him around. Why, the man has gripped his hand. He seems to be a whole lot excited, for he's questioning Fred as if he wanted to make sure everybody was safe out of the cottage."

"I wonder if they are?" remarked Toby. "I've seen little Barbara, and here's our comrade, while I reckon I glimpsed Mrs. Badger over there among those women; but how about the crippled girl, Jack? Anybody seen her around?"

A fresh thrill seized Jack's heart in a grip of ice. Of course it was almost silly to suspect that the cripple could have been forgotten in all the excitement; but anything is liable to happen at a fire, where most people lose their heads, and do things they would call absurd at another time.

"Fred would be apt to know, I should think," suggested Steve, anxiously, casting an apprehensive glance in the direction of the burning house, and mentally calculating just what chance any one still inside those walls would have of coming out alive.

"Unless he was rattled in the bargain," said Jack. "Lots of people leave things for others to do. Fred may have thought his mother would fetch Lucy out; and on her part she took it for granted Fred had taken care of his sister the first thing."

"Gee whiz! I wonder, could that happen, and the poor thing be in there right now," Toby exclaimed, looking horrified at the idea.

"Listen to all that squealing over among the women, will you?" Steve was saying.

Indeed, a fresh outburst of feminine cries could be heard. Apparently something had happened to give the women new cause for fright. Some of those around Fred turned to look. They could see the women running this way and that like a colony of bees that has been disturbed.

"They certain sure act like they might be looking for somebody!" asserted Toby. "See how they ask questions of everyone they meet. Jack, do you think Fred's mother could have just learned that something had happened to her boy; or would it be Lucy they miss for the first time?"

"We'll soon know," said Jack, firmly, "because here comes one of the women running this way like a frightened rabbit."

Eagerly, and with their pulses bounding like mad, they awaited the arrival of the woman. Many others had also turned to greet her, sensing some fresh calamity, before which even the burning of the poor widow's cottage would sink into insignificance.

"Is she here, men?" gasped the woman, almost out of breath. "Have any of you seen Lucy Badger? We can't find her anywhere. Is that Fred there on the ground? He ought to know, because his mother says he must have taken his sister from the house."

They all turned toward Fred. He still sat there looking white and weak, though he was evidently recovering by degrees from his swoon after being hit on the head by some falling object. He looked up in sudden anxiety as he heard the woman speaking.

"What's the matter, Mrs. Moody?" he asked, trying to get on his knees, though the effort was almost too much for his strength. "What's that you said about my sister Lucy? Oh! isn't she with mother and Barbara? I thought sure I saw her in the crowd while I was working trying to save some of the furniture mother valued."

"We can't find the girl anywhere!" the woman cried, in anguish, "and perhaps she's still in there, stupefied by the smoke, and unable to save herself, poor, poor thing. Oh! somebody must try to find out if it's so. Fred, are you able to make the attempt?"

Poor Fred fell back on his knees. His powers of recuperation did not seem equal to the demand. He groaned miserably on discovering how unable he was to doing what in his manly heart he believed to be his solemn duty.

Jack was about to take it upon himself to attempt the dangerous rôle when to his astonishment the mysterious stranger sprang up, and made a thrilling announcement.

CHAPTER XVI
A STARTLING DISCLOSURE

"Let me try to save the child; it is no more than right that I should be the one to risk his life!"

Possibly some of the men might have laid hands on the stranger and prevented his attempting such a rash act, for with the house so filled with smoke and flame it seemed next door to madness for any one to brave the peril that lay in wait. He managed to elude them, however, and to the astonishment of the three boys in particular, plunged recklessly through the door where vast columns of smoke could be seen pouring forth.

Apparently one of the valiant firemen might have been better fitted for this dangerous duty than a gentleman of his calibre. Jack was tempted to follow after the stranger, but the firemen had formed a line in front of the entrance, and by their manner announced that no second fool would be allowed to take his life in his hands by entering that blazing building.

Just then Mrs. Baxter came staggering up. She must have seen the little episode, and suspected strongly that the one who had gone in was her own boy Fred, unable to hold himself in check after learning that his poor sister was in all probability still within the cottage.

Some of the men caught her as she was trying to rush toward the door, holding out her arms entreatingly. The boys understood when they heard her crying:

"Oh! why did you let him go in there? Was it not enough that I should lose one of my children, but now I am doubly bereft! Fred, Fred, come back to me!"

"Mother, see here I am!" called the boy, this time managing to regain his feet, though he swayed unsteadily, and might have fallen in his weakness only for Jack, who quickly put a sustaining arm around him.

Mrs. Badger turned swiftly and with a look of new-born joy on her strained features. Another instant and she had darted forward and embraced Fred. The poor woman was almost frantic with mingled emotions, nor could any one blame her for giving way to weeping as she hugged Fred.

"Oh! I was sure it must be you, my son, and I feared I should never see either of you again!" she cried, passionately.

"I wanted to go, mother," he told her, soothingly, "but I couldn't stand alone. You see, I was struck on the head and knocked out, so I'm feeling as weak as a kitten."

"But Lucy?" wailed the poor woman.

"Try to calm yourself, mother," urged Fred, stoutly. "If she is in there still he may yet be in time to save her, with the aid of Providence."

"But tell me who was so ready to take his own life in his hands, so as to try and save my child for me?" she went on, almost hysterically. "Oh! I shall never cease to remember him for a noble man in my prayers. What neighbor could have been such a Good Samaritan to me and mine!"

"It was the stranger, Mrs. Badger!" said one of the men close by, and Jack, as well as Toby listened eagerly for what was coming.

"Yes, a party who's been hanging around town for a week or more, stopping at the Eureka House," added another of the citizens, who apparently had noticed the presence of the guest in question, and even speculated as to his object in staying so long in Chester, where there were no special summer attractions outside of the beautiful lake near by.

"And he seemed to have lots of money in the bargain," a third went on to say, as he eyed the burning house as though wondering greatly why a stranger would accept such grave risks for people whom he could never have seen before.

"Mebbe I might throw a little light on this thing," said another man, eagerly. "I happened to get in conversation with the party at one time. He goes by the name of Smith at the hotel. He told me he'd been pretty much of a wanderer, and had seen most of the world. But among other things he said was that once on a time he had been a fireman. He even showed me a scar that he said reminded him of a night when he nigh lost his life in a big blaze. So you see he's right in his line when he goes into a burning building to effect a rescue!"

Jack was picking up points as he listened to these things so hurriedly said. He turned to see what effect they had upon Fred and his mother. The woman seemed more bewildered than ever. Evidently she could not understand why a total stranger should risk his life for her child when so many of her neighbors stood around; unless it might be the old fever still burned in Smith's veins, and he could not resist the lure of the crackling flames that seemed to be defying him.

Fred, however, did not look at all puzzled. There was an eager light in his eyes that Jack began to understand. Fred knew something that his mother was utterly ignorant of. He had heard those words of hers about remembering the gallant stranger in her prayers with considerable emotion. Jack even thought the expression written on the face of the boy might spell delight.

"But even if he had at one time been a fire-fighter in the city," Mrs. Badger kept on saying, wonderingly, "why should he be so eager to throw away his life in *my* service. What could a poor woman and her crippled child be to him?"

Then Fred, unable longer to keep his wonderful secret, burst out:

"Oh! mother, don't you know, can't you guess who he is? Why, it's only right he should be the one to save our poor Lucy, or perish in the attempt; because this is the great chance he's been praying would come, so he could prove to you that he has redeemed the past. Mother, surely now you know who he is?"

She stared at him as though bewildered. Then her eyes again sought the burning building into which the stranger had plunged, bent on his mission of mercy. By now the staggering truth must have forced itself into her groping mind, for she suddenly caught hold of Fred again, and hugged him passionately.

"It must be the mysterious ways of Heaven!" Jack heard her say. "Tell me, boy, do you mean that it is—"

"Yes, my father!" Fred said, "and for a whole week and more I have known about his being here. He wanted to wait until I could get up courage enough to break the news to you. He has changed, mother, oh! so much, and made a fortune honestly in the mines, just to show you that the past has been wiped out. And surely this last act of his proves it."

The poor woman sank on her knees. Jack could see her lips move, though of course he was unable to catch a single word she uttered; but he felt positive she was sending up a prayer of gratitude, and beseeching Providence that the precious lives of both father and daughter might be spared through a miracle.

It was all as clear as daylight to Jack now. He could easily understand how at some time in the past, while the Badgers lived in another town, the husband and father had fallen into evil ways, almost breaking his wife's heart. Finally he had possibly been forced to flee from the law, which he may have broken while under the influence of liquor. And all through the years that had come and gone they had never heard of him again, so that she felt she had a right to call herself a widow.

Then one day had come this stranger to Chester, whom Fred must have met, to learn that the other was his own father. He doubtless had been old enough to understand how cruelly his beloved mother had been treated in the past, and it took time to make the boy believe in the protestations of the prodigal father. As the days passed he saw the other frequently, and was gradually coming to believe that his reformation had been sincere.

All the while Mr. Badger had been afraid lest his wife refuse to forgive him, and receive him. From afar he had taken to watching the humble cottage home in which his dear ones dwelt, and doubtless each day saw his yearning to embrace them grow stronger.

Why, Jack could easily understand now his peculiar actions at the time he stood leaning on the picket fence, and watching; also why he should seek to hold the trusting little hand of pretty Barbara as he walked at her side. He would doubtless have given worlds just then for the privilege of clasping the child in his arms and straining her to his heart, but he did not dare, lest she repulse him.

It was simply grand, and Jack's heart beat tumultuously as he watched Mrs. Badger praying for the safety of little Lucy, yes, and also for the life of the man whom she had for years been trying to put out of her mind as utterly unworthy of remembrance.

Just then in the light of his noble sacrifice she undoubtedly forgot all the misery he had caused her during their married life, and could only think of him as he had appeared during their courtship, when she believed him the best of his sex.

It would be all right, Jack believed, if only Mr. Badger might find his Lucy, and be able to save her life. His wife would be only too ready and willing to let the bitter past sink into oblivion, and begin life anew, in her belief in his reformation.

So all interest now hung over the burning cottage. Somewhere inside those doomed walls the man who had once upon a time in his checkered career served as a fireman on a city force, was groping his way about, seeking to stumble over the unconscious form of the poor little cripple whom the pungent smoke had caused to collapse before she could creep to safety.

His utter ignorance of the interior of the cottage would be against him, Jack feared. He wondered whether a double tragedy might complete this wonderful happening; or would Heaven be so kind as to allow the repentant man to save Lucy, and thus again cement the bonds his wickedness in the past had severed?

The only things in his favor were first of all the fact that he had had much experience along this line of life-saving, and would know just how to go about it; and then again his great enthusiasm might serve to carry him along through difficulties that would have daunted most men.

The firemen could do next to nothing to assist in the rescue. They gathered before the building, and sent several streams of water in at the gaping front door, as if desirous of keeping the flames back as long as possible, and thus affording the stranger a better chance for effecting his purpose.

Already he had been inside for several minutes. Events had occurred with lightning-like rapidity, for Fred and his mother had talked eagerly. To Jack, however, it seemed as though a quarter of an hour must have elapsed, he was in such a state of suspense. He felt as though he must break through the line of fire fighters and dash into the cottage, to find the pair they knew to be still there amidst that terrible smoke, so dense and suffocating.

Would they ever come out, he kept asking himself, as he strained his eyes while looking. When hope was beginning to fade away Jack heard a shout that thrilled him to the core, and made him pluck up new courage.

CHAPTER XVII
FRED RENEWS HIS PLEDGE

"There he is!"

It was this thrilling cry that broke out above the noise of the crackling flames, the spatter of rushing water, and the murmur of many voices.

"And he's got the child with him!" another sharp-eyed onlooker shouted exultantly; for although they knew nothing of the tie that bound the stranger to the crippled girl he had gone to save, they could appreciate the heroism at its true value, and were ready to honor the other for his brave deed.

Staggering forth from the building came the man. He utterly disdained any assistance from the ready firemen, lost in admiration for his courage. They might have deemed him next-door to a fool when he dashed into the building, but now in the light of his astonishing success he was a hero.

Mrs. Badger gave a thrilling cry, and advanced toward the man who bore the cripple in his arms. He was a pitiable sight, for most of his beard and hair had been scorched, and in places doubtless he had received burns more or less serious; but he paid no attention to such things.

"Here is your darling child, Mary; I saved her for you!"

Hardly had Mrs. Badger taken the unconscious girl in her arms when the man sank down at her feet in a dead faint. He had held up through everything until he was able to effect his purpose, and then Nature could stand no more.

Jack bent over him and called for water. He sincerely hoped that it might not be so serious as he feared. The experienced fire-fighter would have known better than to have inhaled any of the flame as he passed through; and apparently from the condition of his clothes he could not have been very seriously burned.

No sooner had cold water been applied to his face and neck than he came to, and persisted in sitting up. His gaze wandered wistfully over to where his wife was bending over the crippled girl so solicitously. Jack knew, however, that no matter if the rescue had been made too late, Mr. Badger had undoubtedly earned a right to the forgiveness of the one whom he had so cruelly wronged in the past.

But it seemed that everything was going to come out all right, for now he saw that the women gathered about the mother and child were looking less alarmed. Undoubtedly Lucy was responding to their efforts at resuscitation. She must have fallen on the floor in such a position as to keep her from inhaling much less smoke than would have been the case had she remained on her feet. The air is always found to be purer near the floor during a fire, as many a person trapped within a burning building has discovered.

Now Mrs. Badger had started back toward the spot where the rescuer lay. Perhaps some appealing word from Fred had caused her to remember what she owed to the savior of her crippled child.

Mr. Badger saw her coming; trust his eager eyes for that. He managed to struggle to his feet, and stood there waiting; but he need not have feared concerning the result. What he had done this night had forever washed out the bitterness of the past. All the former tenderness in her heart toward him was renewed when she hurried up, and taking one solicitous tearful look into his blackened face, threw herself into his arms with a glad cry.

"Oh! Donald, we have lost our little home, but I am the happiest woman on earth this night; for what does that matter when I have found *you* again?"

"Mary, my wife, can you find it in your gentle heart to really forgive me?" Jack heard him ask; not that he meant to play the part of eavesdropper, but he chanced to be very close, and was unable to break away from such an affecting scene.

"Never speak of it again to me," she told him. "It is buried forever, all that is displeasing. We will forget it absolutely. In saving our child you have nobly redeemed yourself in my eyes. I am proud of you, Donald. But oh! I hope your hurts may not be serious."

"They could be ten times as serious and I would glory in them," he was saying as Jack turned away; but he saw the man bend down and tenderly kiss his wife, while her arms were about his neck.

Toby, too, had heard everything. He was the possessor of a very tender heart, and as he trotted off at Jack's side he was making all sorts of queer faces, which the other knew full well were meant to hide the fact that his eyes were swimming in tears, and no boy likes it to be known that he is actually crying.

"Did you ever hear of such a fine thing as that, Jack?" Toby was saying between sniffles. "Why, it just goes away ahead of any story I ever read. Think of that man we believed might be a city sport, bent on bribing Fred to throw the great game, turning out to be his own dad! I reckon he treated his poor wife right mean some years ago, and she's never been able to think of him except as a bad egg. But say, he certainly has come back in the last inning, and carried the game off with a wonderful home-run hit."

"And Toby," remarked the delighted Jack, "we can easily understand now why that man hung around the Badger cottage at the time we discovered him leaning on the picket fence. He was hungering for a sight of his wife's face, and counting the minutes until Fred could find some way to introduce the subject to his mother."

"And then about little Barbara, I rather guess he was taken with her pretty face and quaint speech," continued Toby, reflectively. "Why, at the time he skipped out she could not have been any more than a baby. Well, it's all been a drama equal to anything I ever saw shown in the movies; and in the end everything has come out well. I feel like shouting all the way home, I'm so tickled over it."

"Another thing pleases me," continued Jack. "We needn't be bothering our heads over Fred turning traitor to his team after this."

"That's so!" echoed Steve.

"For one," added Toby, sagaciously, "I've had a hunch, Jack, you never could bring yourself to believe that there was anything about that same affair. In spite of the circumstantial evidence in the case you always kept believing Fred must be innocent. Am I right?"

"Perhaps you are, Toby, but I do confess I was considerably worried. Fred's actions were all so suspicious; and besides, we knew that he had great need for a certain sum of money at home. If ever I allowed myself to fear the worst, at the same time I understood that the temptation was great, because of his love for his mother."

"But it's all going to come out just bully now," laughed Toby. "You both heard what Fred said about his father having made a fortune honestly in the mines, working ever so hard, just to prove to his wife how he had surely reformed, and wanted to show it by deeds. They'll have no need to worry over money matters from this time out. And let's hope the prodigal dad will make everybody so happy that they'll almost be glad he went bad and had to reform."

The other boys had to laugh at Toby's queer way of putting it, but they understood what he meant. The fire was still burning furiously, and despite the efforts of Chester's valiant fighters it seemed disposed to make a clean sweep of the cottage with its contents, all but the few precious heirlooms Fred had been able to drag out in the beginning.

"I certainly do hope, though," Steve thought to say presently, "that Fred won't be so knocked out by his blow on the head, and all this wonderful excitement, as not to be able to play in our big game Saturday."

"Gee whiz! that *would* be a calamity for sure!" exclaimed Toby. "Jack, you wondered whether anything else could happen to give you trouble about your line-up against Harmony, and here it has come along. Better have a little heart-to-heart talk with Fred, and get him to promise not to go back on his old pals; for we certainly couldn't fill the gap at third if he dropped out, not at this late day anyhow."

"I meant to do that without your mentioning it, Toby," responded the other, patting his chum on the shoulder as he spoke. "I'll hang around and try to get a chance to speak with Fred when things simmer down a bit. But I tell you right now that boy isn't the one to go back on his friends. He'll play if he's in fit condition, no matter how his home conditions have altered for the better. Why, he'll be so full of happiness, I reckon, Fred Badger will star through the whole game."

"According to all reports from Harmony," remarked Steve, drily, "we'll be apt to need all the starring we can get. They're working like troopers over there, I'm told, because we threw such a scare in 'em that last game, when we got on to Hendrix, and most knocked him out of the box."

"Well, Chester is going some in the bargain," retorted Toby Hopkins. "We believe our team is ten per cent. better than it was last Saturday. Donohue says he never felt so fit as right now; and every fellow on the nine is standing on his toes, ready to prove to the scoffers of Chester that Jack's team here is the peer of any aggregation in the whole country, not even barring the hitherto invincible Harmony crowd. We've got it in for Hendrix, believe *me*!"

Jack liked to hear such enthusiasm. If every member of the team were as much inspired as Toby seemed to be, they would almost certainly prove unbeatable. With such a spirit to back them up, a ninth inning rally was always a strong possibility.

The fire was now beginning to die down, for the house had been pretty well gutted, and there was little standing save the charred walls. Of course the firemen continued to play the hose upon the smoldering pile, but the picturesque part of the conflagration was over, and many people had already commenced to start back home.

Numerous neighbors had offered the family temporary accommodations, and insisted on them coming to stay until they could secure fresh quarters. Perhaps these offers were all of them wholly sincere, though it would perhaps have been only human for some of the good women to be a bit curious concerning the unexpected appearance of Mr. Badger on the scene, whom they had all believed to be dead; and they might relish hearing about the family reunion; though Jack could well believe little would ever be told reflecting on the good name of the repentant husband and father.

He managed to find a chance to speak with Fred, and the squeeze of his hand told the other how much Jack sympathized with him, as well as rejoiced over the happy ending of all Fred's troubles.

"Will I stand by you fellows, and work in that game, are you asking me, Jack?" he ejaculated, presently, when the captain had found a chance to put his question. "Why, wild horses couldn't drag me away from that baseball field. This glorious thing that has come to my dear mother and the rest of us just makes me feel like I could perform better than ever in my life. Make up your mind, Jack, old fellow, Little Fred will be on guard at that third sack on Saturday, barring accidents, and trying to put up the game of his young life. Why, I'm just bubbling over with joy; and I feel like I ought to do my little part toward putting Chester on the map as a center for all boys' sports."

And when later on Jack wended his way toward home, accompanied by Toby and Steve, he felt more positive than ever that a great future was beginning to loom up for the boys of Chester; and the winning of the coming contest would be a gateway leading into the Land of Promise.

CHAPTER XVIII
HENDRIX AGAIN IN THE BOX

On Friday there was a light fall of rain that gave the boys of Chester a fear lest the great game be postponed. It turned out that this was a needless scare, for Saturday opened with fair skies, while even the air seemed delightful for a day in the middle of summer, with a gentle breeze blowing from the west.

The exodus began early in the day, and after noon traffic along the main road leading to Harmony was exceedingly heavy, all sorts of vehicles rolling onward, from sporty cars and laden motor trucks, down to humble wagons and buggies, with plenty of bicycles and motorcycles in evidence.

Once they arrived at the Harmony Field Club grounds, they found that there was to be a most amazing crowd of people to cheer the respective teams on with all manner of encouraging shouts and class yells.

There would not be any change in the line-up of Chester, for luckily all the boys had come through the grilling work of the past week without encountering any serious injuries. Harmony had not been quite so lucky, for their efficient third baseman, Young, had had his collarbone fractured during practice, and would be incapacitated from service the balance of the season.

In his place, a fellow by the name of Parsons was expected to guard third. None of the Chester boys remembered ever having seen him work, so they were utterly in the dark as to his abilities. The Harmony fellows gave out mysterious hints about the "great find" they had made in picking up Parsons, who was a most terrific batter, as well as a dandy third-sacker. He was very likely, they claimed, to break up the whole game by his way of slamming out three-baggers every time he stepped up to bat.

Of course few Chester boys really believed all this high talk. They understood very well that if a weakness had really developed in Harmony's infield, it would be policy on the part of the local rooters to try to conceal the fact, so that the Chester batters might not focus all their hits in the direction of third. Nevertheless, the boasting of the Harmony fans gave more than one visitor a cold feeling around the region of his heart. He watched Parsons in the practice before the game was called, and every little stunt which he performed was horribly magnified in their eyes.

Fortunately, Mr. Merrywether, the impartial umpire, was able to officiate again, which fact pleased both sides. They knew they could be sure of a square deal at his hands, and that was all any honest ball player could ask. When the public understands that an umpire always tries to do his duty as he sees it, and cannot be swerved from his path by any hoodlum tactics, they seem to feel a sort of affection for such a man, who is an honor to his chosen profession.

Long before the time came for play to begin every seat was taken, and hundreds were standing; while every avenue leading to the enclosed grounds seemed to be choked with hurrying, jostling throngs. They were anxious to at least get within seeing distance of the diamond, where they could add their voices to the cheers bound to arise as brilliant plays were pulled off by either side.

This was certainly the biggest event in the line of boys sports that had ever occurred at or near Harmony. Such a vast outpouring of people had never before been seen. Chester was represented by hundreds of her best citizens, attended by their wives. And really it would be hard to think of a Chester boy over ten years of age who had not managed somehow or other to get over, so as to watch how Jack Winters and his team came out in the conclusive game with the great Hendrix.

All species of noises arose all around the field, from a myriad of automobile horns and frequent school yells given under the direction of the rival cheer captains, who stood in front of the bleachers, and waved their arms like semaphores as they led their cohorts in concert, whooping out the recognized yells of either Harmony or Chester.

The pitchers were trying out in one corner of the grounds in full view of the entire mass of spectators. Many curious eyes watched them limber up their arms for the work before them. Besides Hendrix and Donohue several reserve pitchers on either side were in line, sending and receiving in routine; but of course never once delivering their deceptive curves or drops, lest the opposing players get a line on their best tricks, and prepare to meet them later on.

No one had any doubts concerning who was slated to occupy the box. It was bound to be the same batteries as in the last game, Hendrix and Chase for Harmony, Donohue and Mullane for Chester. If for any reason either of these star pitchers should be so unfortunate as to get a "lacing," then possibly one of the substitutes might be introduced so as to save the day; but there was a slim chance of any such thing coming to pass.

Jack had no reason to feel discouraged. To be sure, he had passed through quite a strenuous week, and been worried over a number of his leading players; but after all, things had turned out very well. Now that the great day had arrived, he believed every fellow on the nine was feeling first class.

There was Donohue, for instance, who had been on the verge of throwing up his job as pitcher because he believed he would be over in Harmony when the day arrived, living there for good; but Jack had fixed all that, so that he was now firmly settled as a citizen of Chester, and could put his whole heart into his work in the box.

Joel Jackman had come close to drowning, but it was Jack who had been instrumental in rescuing him when he caught that cramp in the cold water of the lake; and, so far as appearances went, Joel was feeling as he declared, "just prime." He ran after the loftiest flies that were knocked his way as though he had the speed of the wind; yes, and not once was he guilty of a flagrant muff, though some of those balls called for an exhibition of agility and skill bordering on genius.

Lastly, there was Fred Badger, who had also given Jack many a heartache since the last tie game with Harmony; but Fred was jumping around his favorite third sack, smothering every grounder that sped his way, and pegging to first with a promptness and accuracy that made some of the Harmony fans shiver as they thought of how easily their fastest runner would be caught miles from the base by such wonderful playing as that, provided Fred could do as well in the real game.

The time was close at hand for the umpire to call play, and of course there was an eagerness as well as a tinge of anxiety running through the crowds of spectators. In a hotly contested game such as was very likely to develop, often a little thing will seem like a mountain; and upon a mere trifle the fate of the contest may in the end depend. Should any one of the players "crack" under the strain, such a thing was likely to settle the controversy for good.

Since there was such a monstrous crowd present that ropes had to be used to keep them from surging on to the field, of course ground rules had to be arranged in advance. This was certain to work a little in favor of the home team. For instance, every Harmony batter knew that a hit toward right would send the ball into the near bleachers, which feat would count for two bases; whereas, if the ball were free to travel, it might be fielded back in time to hold the runner at first. Then again, a little more steam would send the horse-hide careening over right-field fence for a home-run. Doubtless Harmony batters had practiced for just such special hits many, many times; whereas, the Chester fellows, being almost green to the grounds, would be apt to hit as they were accustomed to doing at home.

Jack, like a wise general, saw this opening, and one of the first things he did in giving counsel to his players was to point it out to Big Bob Jeffries, Joel Jackman, Steve Mullane and the rest of the heavy sluggers.

"Start them for right field every time you can, boys," he advised. "It doesn't take so much of a tap to put them across the fence there; and if you can't get so far land a few in the bleachers for a double."

"How about the third sack, Jack?" asked Phil Parker. "You know I'm a great hand to knock across the line there. Some get into foul territory, passing outside the bag; but when they do go over squarely they always count for keeps. Do you believe half they're saying about that Parsons being a regular demon for grabbing up ground scorchers, and tossing fellows out at first?"

"None of us will know until we make the test," Jack told him. "Start things up lively for Mr. Parsons the first time you face Hendrix, Phil. If we find he's all to the good there, we'll change off, and ring in a new deal. But somehow I seem to have a sneaking notion that same Parsons will turn out to be the Harmony goat in this game. They've done their best to replace Young; and now hope to hide the truth by all this bragging."

"I wouldn't be at all surprised if what you say turns out to be a fact, Jack," remarked Steve. "You know we read a whole lot these days about the war over in Europe, and how the French have a masterly way of hiding their big guns under a mattress of boughs, or a painted canvas made to represent the earth, so that flying scouts above can't see where the battery is located. Well, perhaps now Harmony, in making all this brag is only trying to hide their gap. Camaflouge they call it, I believe. But we'll proceed to see what Parsons has got up his sleeve. You watch me get him to guessing. If he gets in the way of the cannonball I shoot at third, it'll feel like a hot tamale in his hands, believe me."

"Well, there's Mr. Merrywether going to announce the batteries, and so we'll have a chance to see what we can do at bat, for of course Harmony takes the field first. Every fellow fight tooth and nail for Chester. We want to go home this afternoon in a blaze of glory. Win or lose, we must show that we are a credit to our folks. That's all I've got to say as a last word; every fellow on his toes every second of the time, at bat, and in the field!"

The umpire raised his voice, and using a megaphone proceeded to announce that the opposing batteries of the two rival teams would be:

"Hendrix and Chase for Harmony; Donohue and Mullane for Chester!"

A storm of approval greeted the announcement. Everybody settled back as though relieved, and confident that no matter who won, they would see a game well worth patronizing.

Hendrix received the new ball, and proceeded to send a few swift ones to his basemen. They of course managed to drop it on the ground as often as they could, so that it might be dextrously rolled a bit, and discolored, for it is always considered that a new ball works in favor of the batter.

Jack was the first man to face Hendrix, as he led the batting list. From all over the place loud cries greeted the captain of the Chester team as he stepped up to the plate, and stood there with his bat on his shoulder. Of course most of these encouraging cries came from the faithful Chester rooters; but then there were fair-minded fellows of Harmony who believed in giving due credit to an honorable antagonist; and Jack Winters they knew to be such a type of boy, clean in everything he attempted, and a true lover of outdoor sports.

"Play ball!"

Hendrix took one last look all around. He wished to make sure that his fielders and basemen were just as he would have them placed. He knew that Jack could wield a bat with considerable skill; and moreover had proved his ability to solve his delivery on that former occasion. So proceeding to wind up he sent in the first one with sizzling speed, and a sharp drop.

CHAPTER XIX
THE LUCKY SEVENTH

"Strike One!" announced the wideawake umpire, in his stentorian voice.

Subdued applause ran through the immense throng. Apparently Hendrix had perfect control over the ball. That wonderful drop had been too quick for Jack, who, considering that it was entirely too high, had not struck. Perhaps, though, he was waiting to see what Hendrix meant to feed him.

The next one went wide in a curve that elicited murmurs of admiration from the sages of the ball game, who invariably insisted on sitting in a direct line with catcher and pitcher, their one occupation being to gauge the delivery, and shout out approval or disdain over every ball that comes along; or else plague the umpire because his decision differs from their wonderful judgment.

Then came the third toss. Jack stepped forward, and before the break could occur he had met the twisting ball with the point of his bat, sending it humming down toward short.

Bailey was on his job, and neatly smothered what might have been a splendid single. When Jack reached first after a speedy rush, he found the ball there ahead of him gripped in Hutching's fist, and was greeted with a wide grin from the astute first baseman.

"One down!" remarked Toby Hopkins, as Phil Parker toed the mark, and watched the opposing pitcher like a hawk, meaning to duplicate Jack's feat if possible, only he aspired to send the ball through the infield, and not straight at a man.

"But Jack got at him, you noticed," said Joel Jackman, who did not seem to be showing any signs of his recent adventure in the chilly waters of the lake. "Hendrix may be a puzzle to a good many fellows, but once you solve his tricks well, say, he's as easy as pie at Thanksgiving."

Well, Joel had a chance that very inning to show what he meant, for while Phil reached first on a Texas leaguer, and Herbert Jones whiffed vainly at three balls that came over the plate with lightening speed, there were only two out.

Joel made a swing at a wide one on purpose, for he had received the signal from Phil that he meant to make a break for second when next Hendrix started to wind up to deliver the ball. Luck was with Phil, thanks partly to the great slide with which he covered the last ten feet of ground; and also to the fact that the generally reliable Chase, Harmony's backstop, managed to draw the second baseman off his bag to stop his speedy throw.

Hendrix showed no signs of being alarmed. He tempted Joel to take a chance at a most deceptive drop, which put the batter two in the hole with just as many balls called on the box-man.

With the next toss, Joel, meaning to emulate Jack's manner of stepping forward and meeting the ball before the break came, entirely miscalculated Hendrix' scheme. As a consequence, the ball, instead of being a sharp drop, seemed to actually *rise* in the air, and in consequence, Joel missed it by half a foot.

He went to his position out in centre, fastening his glove, and shaking his head.

"How'd you find Hendrix today, Joel?" asked Oldsmith, the Harmony middle-field man, as they passed on the way. "Some stuff he's got on that ball, hey?"

"That last was certainly a new one for me," confessed Joel, frankly. "Why, honest to goodness, it seemed to jump up in the air just before I swung."

"Sure, that's the new jump ball he's been practicing lately," grinned Oldsmith, though whether he really believed such a thing himself or not was a question, for he seemed to be a practical joker. "Old Hendrix is always hatching up something fresh, for the other side. You fellows needn't expect to do much running today, for most of you will only whiff out at the rubber. He's got your number, all right."

Of course that did not bother Joel very much. He knew how prone baseball players are to boast when things are turning their way; and at the same time find all sorts of plausible excuses when the reverse tide begins to flow against them.

Donohue seemed to be at his best, for he immediately struck out the first man who faced him, tossing up just three balls at that. This was quite a creditable performance the Chester rooters kept telling their Harmony neighbors, considering that he was no veteran at this sort of thing, and Hutchings could usually be counted on as a dependable hitter.

Clifford fared but little better, though it was through a lofty foul to right field which Big Bob easily smothered, that he went out. Then

Captain Martin tried his hand, and he, too, seemed unable properly to gauge the teasers that Donohue sent in, for after fouling several, he passed away on the third strike.

The crowd made up its mind that it was going to be a pitchers' duel in earnest. Many would go the way of those who had been unable to meet the puzzling curves and drops that had come in by turns.

When next the Chester boys tried their hand, Toby got his base through Parsons juggling the hot grounder which came his way, and failing to send it across the diamond in time to nip the runner. The Chester folks took notice of this error on the part of the third baseman, who had been touted as a wonder at snatching up everything that came his way, regardless of its character. Still, that had been a difficult ball to handle, and the error was excusable, Jack thought.

There was no run made, though Big Bob did send out a terrific drive that under ordinary conditions should have been a three-bagger at least. Oldsmith, after a gallant sprint at top speed, was seen to jump into the air and pull the ball down. He received a storm of applause, for it was a pretty piece of work; and Chester fans cheered quite as lustily as the home crowd; for, as a rule, baseball rooters can admire such splendid results regardless of partisanship.

Badger struck out, in his turn, being apparently unable to solve those puzzling shoots of the cool and smiling master in the box. But then Harmony was no better off in their half of that inning, for not a man got as far as second; though O'Leary did send up an amazing fly that dropped squarely in the hands of Big Bob. The other two only smashed the thin air when they struck, for they picked out wide ones, and let the good balls shoot over the edges of the plate like cannonballs.

"Notice one thing," said Jack to several of the Chester players when once more it was their turn at bat. "Every Harmony fellow turns partly toward the right when he bats. That's the short field in this enclosure, and with the bleachers in between. They know the advantages of sending the ball in that direction every time it's possible. Phil, Joel and Bob, make a note of that, will you, and try to duplicate their game? They know the grounds, and have the advantage over us."

"Watch my smoke, Governor," chuckled Big Bob Jeffries, confidently. "I'm only trying things out so far. When the right time comes, me to cash in with a ball clean over that short field fence. They'll never find it again either, if I get the swoop I'm aiming for."

"Well, use good judgment when you make it," laughed Jack, "and see that the bases are occupied. We may need a homer before this gruelling game is over."

It certainly began to look like it when the sixth inning had ended and never a run was marked up on the score-board for either side. Once Fred Badger had succeeded in straining a point, and reaching third with a wonderful exhibition of base stealing; but alas! he died there. Steve, usually so reliable, could not bring him in, though he did valiantly, and knocked a sky-scraper which O'Leary scooped in after a run back to the very edge of the bleachers. Five feet further and it would have dropped safe, meaning a two-bagger for Steve, and a run for Badger.

So the seventh started. Both pitchers were going as strong as in the start, even more so, many believed. It was a wonderful exhibition of skill and endurance, and thousands were ready to declare that no such game had ever been played upon the grounds of the Harmony Field Club.

"Everybody get busy this frame," said Jack, encouragingly, as Donohue picked up a bat and strode out to take his place. "We've got to make a start some time, and the lucky seventh ought to be the right place. Work him for a walk if you can Alec. And if you get to first, we'll bat you in, never fear."

Considerably to the surprise of everybody, Donohue, instead of striking out, managed to connect with a swift ball, and send up a weak fly that fell back of second. Three players started for it, but there must have been some fierce misunderstanding of signals, for they all stopped short to avoid a collision, each under the belief that one of the others had cried he had it. In consequence, the ball fell to the ground safely, and the Chester pitcher landed on the initial sack.

Such roars as went up from the faithful and expectant Chester rooters. They managed to make such a noise that one would have been pardoned for thinking the entire crowd must be in sympathy with the visitors. Anticipation jumped to fever heat. With a runner located on first base, no one out, and several reliable batters coming up, it began to look as though that might yet prove the "lucky seventh" for the plucky Chester boys.

Jack knew that Hendrix would have it in for him. He would depend on sweeping curves that must deceive, and try no more of that drop ball, which Jack had proved himself able to judge and meet before it broke.

So Jack, after one swing at a spinner which he did not expect to strike, dropped a neat little bunt along the line toward first. This allowed the runner to reach second, although Jack himself was caught; for Hendrix instantly darted over to first, and was in time to receive the ball after Hatchings had scooped it out of the dirt.

But the runner had been advanced to second, and there were still two chances that he could be sent on his way by a mighty wallop, or even a fine single. Phil did crack out one that did the trick, and he found himself landed on first, though Donohue, unfortunately, was held at third. Bedlam seemed to be breaking loose. Chester rooters stormed and cheered, and some of the more enthusiastic even danced around like maniacs. Others waited for something really to be accomplished before giving vent to their repressed feelings.

Next up stepped Herb Jones, with a man on third, another on first, and but a lone out. He failed to accomplish anything, Hendrix sending him along by the usual strike-out line.

Everything depended on Joel. A single was all that was needed to bring in the tally so ardently desired. It was no time to try for a big hit. Even Phil on first was signaled not to take risks in starting for second.

Joel waited. He was fed a couple of wide ones that the umpire called balls. Then came a fair one clean across the rubber, but Joel did not strike. Jack made a motion to him. He believed the next would also be a good ball, for Hendrix was not likely to put himself in a hole right there, depending more on his dazzling speed to carry him through.

Joel struck!

They heard the crack of the bat, but few saw the ball go, such was its momentum as it passed through the diamond. Hendrix, however, made a stab with his glove and managed to deflect the ball from its first course. That turned out to be a fatal involuntary movement on his part, for it made Bailey's job in knocking down the ball more difficult. The nimble shortstop managed to recover the ball and send it in home; but as the runner at third had of course started tearing along as he heard the blow, he had slid to safety before Chase caught the throw in.

And so the first tally of the game fell to Chester in the lucky seventh!

CHAPTER XX
AFTER THE GREAT VICTORY–CONCLUSION

Toby Hopkins made a gallant effort to duplicate the performance of some of his mates. He cracked out a dandy hit well along toward the bleachers out in right field. Again did O'Leary run like mad, or a "red-headed meteor," as some of his admirers yelled. They saw him actually leap amidst the bleachers, the spectators giving way like frightened sheep. Yes, and he caught that fly in a most amazing fashion, well deserving the loud salvos of cheers that kept up as he came in, until he had doffed his cap in response to the mad applause.

But Harmony came back in their half of the seventh with a tally that resulted from a screaming hit by the hero of the game, O'Leary, which carried far over the famous right-field fence.

With the score thus evened up, they went at the eighth frame. Big Bob got a single out in right. He was advanced to second by a fine bunt on the part of Fred Badger, which the new third baseman found it difficult to handle, though he did succeed in nailing the runner at first. Along came Steve with a zigzag hit that made a bad bound over shortstop's head and allowed Big Bob to land on third. He was kept from going home by the coacher there, who saw that Oldsmith had dashed in from short center, and was already picking up the ball for a throw home, which he did with fine judgment.

Donohue was unable to duplicate his previous lucky pop-up, for he struck out. Jack was given his base on balls, an unusual occurrence with Hendrix. Apparently, however, he was banking on being better able to strike out Phil Parker, which he immediately proceeded to do, so that after all, the Chester rally did not net a run, and the score was still a tie.

Chester went to the field for the finish of the eighth, determined that there should be no let down of the bars. Jack had spoken encouraging words to Donohue, and was confidently told by the pitcher that he felt as "fresh as a daisy, with speed to burn."

He proved the truth of his words immediately by striking out the first man to face him. Then the next Harmony batter managed to send up several high fouls that kept Big Bob in right hustling; though he finally succeeded in getting hold of one, and putting the man out.

The third batter hit the ball with fierceness, but Jack took it for a line drive, and that inning was over. The ninth was looming up and the game still undecided. Indeed, they were no better off than when making the start, save that they had had considerable practice whiffing the thin air.

"You see, they persist in trying to drive toward right," urged Jack, as his players came trooping in, eager to get busy again with their bats, so as to win the game in this ninth round.

"Yes, and they kept me on the jump right smart in the bargain," remarked Big Bob Jeffries, wiping his reeking forehead as he spoke. "Never mind, I'll have a chance at Hendrix again this inning, likely, if one of you fellows can manage to perch on the initial sack. Then watch what happens. I'm going to break up this bally old game right now."

"Deeds talk, Big Bob!" chuckled Toby, as Herb Jones stepped up to see what he could do for a starter.

His best was a foul that the catcher smothered in his big mitt after quite an exciting rush here and there, for it was difficult to judge of such a twister. Herb looked utterly disgusted as he threw down his bat. Joel Jackman struck the first offering dealt out to him, and got away with it in the bargain. Perched on first the lanky fielder grinned, and called out encouragingly at Toby, who was next.

Hendrix tightened up. He looked very grim and determined. Toby wanted to bunt, but he managed instead to send a little grounder along toward first. Joel was already booming along in the direction of second, and taking a grand slide, for fear that the throw would catch him.

But after all Chase had some difficulty in picking up the ball, as sometimes happens to the best of them; and while he did hurl it to second, the umpire held up his hands to announce that Joel was safe. No one disputed his decision, though it had been a trifle close.

Matters were looking up for Chester again. One man was down, but that was Big Bob Jeffries striding up to the plate, with a grim look on his face. If Hendrix were wise he would send him along on balls; but then the pitcher had perfect faith in his ability to deceive the heaviest of hitters.

Twice did Big Bob swing, each time almost falling down when his bat met with no resistance. He took a fresh grip and steeled himself. Jack called out a word of warning, but Big Bob shook his head. No matter what Hendrix gave him, he could reach it, his confident, almost bulldog manner declared.

Well, he did!

He smacked the very next offering of the great Harmony pitcher so hard that it looked like a dot in the heavens as it sped away over right-field fence for a magnificent home run.

Big Bob trotted around the circuit with a wide grin on his face, chasing Joel and Toby before him, while the crowd went fairly wild with joy—at least that section of it representative of Chester did. The Harmony rooters looked pretty blue, to tell the truth, for they realized that only a miracle could keep their rivals from running off with the hard-fought game.

"That sews it up, I reckon!" many of them were heard to say.

There were no more runs made by Chester, for Hendrix mowed the next batter down with comparative ease; but the mischief had already been done.

Harmony made a last fierce effort to score in their half of the ninth. Chase got his base on balls, and Hendrix tried to advance him with a sacrifice, but succeeded only in knocking into a double. Then Hutchings cracked out a two-sacker, and Clifford came along with a neat single that sent the other runner on to third, while he occupied the initial sack. Harmony stock began to rise. Those who had made a movement as though about to quit their seats sat down again. Possibly the game was not yet over. Some clever work on the part of Martin, Oldsmith and Bailey might tie the score, when, as on the last occasion, extra innings would be necessary in order to prove which of the teams should be awarded the victor's laurel.

Everybody seemed to be rooting when Captain Martin stepped up. He succeeded in picking out a good one, and with the sound of the blow there was an instinctive loud "Oh!" on the part of hundreds. But, alas! for the fate of Harmony! the ball went directly at Fred Badger, who sent it straight home in time to catch Hutchings by seven feet, despite his mad rush.

And so the great game wound up, with the score four to one in favor of Chester. Doubtless, the most depressed member of the defeated Harmony team would be Hendrix, who had failed to baffle those batters with all his wonderful curves and trick drops.

On the way home after the game, with the Chester players occupying a big carryall, their joyous faces told every one along the way how they had fared, even if their shouts failed to announce their victory.

"This is a grand day in the history of Chester," said Jack for the tenth time, since he shared in the enthusiasm that seemed to run through every fellow's veins. "It will be written down as a red letter day by every boy, young and old; for we have put the old town on the baseball map for keeps. After this folks will speak of Chester teams with respect, for we've gallantly downed the champions of the county two to one, with a great tie thrown in for good measure. I want to thank every one of you for what you've done to help out– Phil, Herb, Joel, Toby, Big Bob, Fred, Steve, and last but far from least our peerless pitcher Alec Donohue. Not one of you but played your position to the limit; and as to batting, never this summer has Hendrix had the lacing he got today, so I was privately told by one of the Harmony fans whose money has been back of the team all summer."

"We'll make Rome howl tonight, boys, believe me!" asserted Big Bob. "Bonfires and red lights all over the town, while we march through the streets, and shout till we're hoarse as crows. The like never happened before in Chester, and it's only right the good folks should know we've made the place famous."

"What pleases me most of all," Jack went on to say, when he could find a chance to break into the lively talk, "is the bright prospect that looms up before us. This glorious baseball victory clinches matters. I know several gentlemen who will now be eager to back up our scheme for a club-house this winter, as well as a football eleven to compete for the county championship up to Thanksgiving. And during the balance of the summer I've got a lively programme laid out that ought to give the bunch of us a heap of pleasure, as well as profit us in the way of healthy exercise."

His announcement was greeted with hearty cheers, for they knew full well that when Jack Winters engineered any scheme it was likely to turn out well worth attention. But it would hardly be fair just now to disclose what Jack's plans were; that may well be left to the succeeding volume in this series of athletic achievements on the part of the Chester boys, which can be found wherever juvenile books are sold under the title of "Jack Winters' Campmates; or, Vacation Days in the Woods."

THE END

VICTORY BOY SCOUT SERIES

Stories by a writer who possesses a thorough knowledge of this subject. Handsomely bound in cloth; colored jacket wrapper.

1 The Campfires of the Wolf Patrol
2 Woodcraft; or, How a Patrol Leader Made Good
3 Pathfinder; or, the Missing Tenderfoot
4 Great Hike; or, The Pride of Khaki Troop
5 Endurance Test; or, How Clear Grit Won the Day
6 Under Canvas; or, the Search for the Carteret Ghost
7 Storm-bound; or, a Vacation among the Snow Drifts
8 Afloat; or, Adventures on Watery Trails
9 Tenderfoot Squad; or, Camping at Raccoon Bluff
10 Boy Scouts in an Airship
11 Boy Scout Electricians; or, the Hidden Dynamo
12 Boy Scouts on Open Plains

For Sale by all Book-sellers, or sent postpaid on receipt of 40 cents

M · A · DONOHUE · & · COMPANY

711 SOUTH DEARBORN STREET · · CHICAGO

BOY SCOUT SERIES

By

G. HARVEY RALPHSON

Just the type of books that delight and fascinate the wide awake boys of today. Clean, wholesome and interesting; full of mystery and adventure. Each title is complete and unabridged. Printed on a good quality of paper from large, clear type and bound in cloth. Each book is wrapped in a special multi-colored jacket.

1. Boy Scouts in Mexico; or, On Guard with Uncle Sam
2. Boy Scouts in the Canal Zone; or, the Plot against Uncle Sam
3. Boy Scouts in the Philippines; or, the Key to the Treaty Box
4. Boy Scouts in the Northwest; or, Fighting Forest Fires
5. Boy Scouts in a Motor Boat; or Adventures on Columbia River
6. Boy Scouts in an Airship; or, the Warning from the Sky
7. Boy Scouts in a Submarine; or, Searching an Ocean Floor

8. Boy Scouts on Motorcycles; or, With the Flying Squadron
9. Boy Scouts beyond the Arctic Circle; or, the Lost Expedition
10. Boy Scout Camera Club; or, the Confessions of a Photograph
11. Boy Scout Electricians; or, the Hidden Dynamo
12. Boy Scouts in California; or, the Flag on the Cliff
13. Boy Scouts on Hudson Bay; or, the Disappearing Fleet
14. Boy Scouts in Death Valley; or, the City in the Sky
15. Boy Scouts on Open Plains; or, the Roundup not Ordered
16. Boy Scouts in Southern Waters; or the Spanish Treasure Chest
17. Boy Scouts in Belgium; or, Imperiled in a Trap
18. Boy Scouts in the North Sea; or, the Mystery of a Sub
19. Boy Scouts Mysterious Signal; or, Perils of the Black Bear Patrol
20. Boy Scouts with the Cossacks; or, a Guilty Secret

For Sale by all Book-sellers, or sent postpaid on receipt of 60 cents

M · A · DONOHUE · & · COMPANY

711 SOUTH DEARBORN STREET · · CHICAGO

MOTOR BOAT BOYS SERIES

By Louis Arundel

1. The Motor Club's Cruise Down the Mississippi; or The Dash for Dixie.
2. The Motor Club on the St. Lawrence River; or Adventures Among the Thousand Islands.
3. The Motor Club on the Great Lakes; or Exploring the Mystic Isle of Mackinac.
4. Motor Boat Boys Among the Florida Keys; or The Struggle for the Leadership.
5. Motor Boat Boys Down the Coast; or Through Storm and Stress.
6. Motor Boat Boy's River Chase; or Six Chums Afloat or Ashore.
7. Motor Boat Boys Down the Danube; or Four Chums Abroad

MOTOR MAID SERIES

By Katherine Stokes

1. Motor Maids' School Days
2. Motor Maids by Palm and Pine

4

3. Motor Maids Across the Continent
4. Motor Maids by Rose, Shamrock and Thistle
5. Motor Maids in Fair Japan
6. Motor Maids at Sunrise Camp

For Sale by all Book-sellers, or sent postpaid on receipt of 75c

M · A · DONOHUE · & · COMPANY

711 SOUTH DEARBORN STREET · · CHICAGO

RADIO BOYS SERIES

1. Radio Boys in the Secret Service; or, Cast Away on an Iceberg ... FRANK HONEYWELL
2. Radio Boys on the Thousand Islands; or, The Yankee Canadian Wireless Trail ... FRANK HONEYWELL
3. Radio Boys in the Flying Service; or, Held for Ransom by Mexican Bandits ... J. W. DUFFIELD
4. Radio Boys Under the Sea; or, The Hunt for the Sunken Treasure ... J. W. DUFFIELD
5. Radio Boys Cronies; or, Bill Brown's Radio ... WAYNE WHIPPLE
6. Radio Boys Loyalty; or, Bill Brown Listens In ... WAYNE WHIPPLE

PEGGY PARSON'S SERIES

By Annabel Sharp

A popular and charming series of Girl's books dealing in an interesting and fascinating manner with the the life and adventures of Girlhood so dear to all Girls from eight to fourteen years of age. Printed from large clear type on superior quality paper, multi-color jacket. Bound in cloth.

1. Peggy Parson Hampton Freshman
2. Peggy Parson at Prep School

For Sale by all Book-sellers, or sent postpaid on receipt of 75c

M · A · DONOHUE · & · COMPANY

711 SOUTH DEARBORN STREET · · CHICAGO

THE AEROPLANE SERIES

By John Luther Langworthy

1. The Aeroplane Boys; or, The Young Pilots First Air Voyage
2. The Aeroplane Boys on the Wing; or, Aeroplane Chums in the Tropics
3. The Aeroplane Boys Among the Clouds; or, Young Aviators in a Wreck
4. The Aeroplane Boys' Flights; or, A Hydroplane Round-up
5. The Aeroplane Boys on a Cattle Ranch

THE GIRL AVIATOR SERIES

By Margaret Burnham

Just the type of books that delight and fascinate the wide awake girls of the present day who are between the ages of eight and fourteen years. The great author of these books regards them as the best products of her pen. Printed from large clear type on a superior quality of paper; attractive multi-color jacket wrapper around each book. Bound in cloth.

1. The Girl Aviators and the Phantom Airship
2. The Girl Aviators on Golden Wings
3. The Girl Aviators' Sky Cruise
4. The Girl Aviators' Motor Butterfly.

For Sale by all Book-sellers, or sent postpaid on receipt of 75c

M · A · DONOHUE · & · COMPANY

711 SOUTH DEARBORN STREET · · CHICAGO